W9-AWH-235

WITHDRAWN

The Ham Reporter

The Ham Reporter

Bat Masterson in New York

ROBERT J. RANDISI

DOUBLEDAY & COMPANY, INC.

GARDEN CITY, NEW YORK

1986

With the exception of actual historical persons,
all of the characters in this book
are fictitious, and any resemblance
to actual persons, living or dead,
is purely coincidental.

Library of Congress Cataloging-in-Publication Data

Randisi, Robert J.
The ham reporter.

1. Masterson, Bat, 1853–1921—Fiction. I. Title.
PS3568.A53H3   1986   813'.54   86–2129

ISBN: 0-385-23006-0

For Christopher and Matthew, who inspire me just by being my sons.
And for their mother, Anna, who inspires me just by being.
I love you.

A sportswriter who is not willing to stand by his honest judgment . . . ought to chuck his job and try something else. . . . The fight reviewer who lacks the knack of drawing imaginary pictures and incidents that did not exist and tossing them into the story of a frame is promptly set down by the reading public as a ham reporter. I am a ham of the most pronounced type.

—Bat Masterson, July 5, 1921
The New York Morning Telegraph

The Ham Reporter

Prologue

New York
October 1911

"The Pueblo Fireman" had never thrown a fight before, but to Jim Flynn seventy-five hundred dollars seemed like a lot of money to turn down on principle.

"It's a tidy sum, Jim," Texas oilman Frank Ufer said, as if reading the fighter's mind.

Flynn agreed.

Ufer shook the bundle of banded bills in his hand, thinking what a fool the other man was not to hold out for more. Ufer could well afford more—even if he *hadn't* stood to make ten times as much on the fight—but if he could get Flynn that cheap, why not?

Without this buy-off he knew that his man, Carl Morris, stood little or no chance at all against the more experienced Flynn. He shook the bills again, practically under the other man's nose, enjoying the sound they made when they rubbed up against each other.

"You could do a lot of things with seventy-five hundred dollars, Jimmy-boy." Ufer's tone was seductive.

Flynn's eyes never left the money as he nodded in agreement. Yeah, he thought, he sure could do a lot. . . .

Ufer made his final move, the one he knew would clinch the deal. He made as if to put the money away in the pocket of his expensively cut jacket where it had appeared from, and the move galvanized Flynn into action. His right hand shot out and snatched the money out of Ufer's grasp.

"Done!" Ufer cried out triumphantly.

"Yeah," Flynn said, staring down at the packet of money that now lay in *his* hand. He was still not convinced that he had done the right thing.

"All right, my boy, all right." Ufer slapped the younger man on the back heartily. "We'll be seeing you at the Garden, then, eh?"

"Yes, sir."

"Be in shape, boy, you've got to make it look good. I'd like the fight to go at least ten or twelve rounds."

Even as he said this Ufer hoped that his man, the loutish, lumbering Carl Morris, wouldn't have fallen down exhausted by that time.

"Better make it eight or nine rounds, Jimmy," he said, reconsidering. "No sense taking any chances."

"Sure, Mr. Ufer, sure." Jim Flynn did not look like a man who had just made seventy-five hundred dollars, nor did he sound like one. He was positively glum as he said, "It'll look good."

Ufer hoped the man would keep his end of the bargain and not give in to an attack of guilt. Why, he wouldn't make seventy-five hundred dollars fighting the champ himself!

"Fine, fine," Ufer said. "I'd better leave first, then." He patted Flynn on the shoulder again and said, "You've made the right decision, my boy. It would take you a lot of lumps to make that much money in the ring otherwise."

"Sure, Mr. Ufer."

Ufer left the back room of the small Fourteenth Street restaurant and proceeded through the main dining area to the front door. He was intercepted there by Lou Kramer, Herman Rosenthal's right-hand man.

"How did it go?" Kramer asked.

"It went fine, Kramer, just fine. Just like I said it would. The kid couldn't turn down the money." Ufer was rubbing his hands together with glee.

"That's good," Kramer said, although from the look on his face one wouldn't think it was so. However, Ufer knew that Kramer's facial expression rarely changed from the dour look it now wore.

"That's *real* good," Kramer said again, looking down at the smaller Ufer. Rosenthal's man was a huge hulk with sloping shoulders and heavy features, and it struck Ufer that this was probably what Carl Morris would look like in ten years or so. "Mr. Rosenthal will be pleased."

"Of course he will," Ufer said, looking up at the large man nervously.

"If nothing goes wrong."

"What could go wrong?"

"Mr. Rosenthal doesn't like to lose."

"He won't, I promise you that. It's all fixed."

Kramer leaned over Ufer and said, "I'll tell him you said so."

"I'll be seeing you, Kramer," Ufer said, stepping past the big man. "If you're smart, you'll place a substantial bet yourself."

"I don't gamble."

"No," Ufer said, "you wouldn't."

Ufer hurried out to his buggy. Although he had plenty of money and could have afforded an automobile, he disdained the things, thinking them filthy and disgusting. He thought even less of the taximeter cabs which had been imported from France in 1907, and would not have been caught dead riding New York's subway system. Traveling underground was for animals, not for men—especially men of his means.

He climbed into his buggy and told his driver, "Back to the Hotel Deleran."

"Yes, sir."

The driver was his lackey, just as Lou Kramer was Herman Rosenthal's lackey. Ufer became angry with himself every time he started feeling afraid of Kramer, but he couldn't help himself. He'd heard stories of the things Kramer could do to a man with his bare hands, and then of course there was the power of Rosenthal behind the man.

He shuddered as, unbidden, the vision of Kramer lifting him up in his massive hands came to him, and he huddled in a corner of the buggy, trying in vain to hide from the thought.

(2)

Lou Kramer said nothing to Flynn as the pugilist left the restaurant moments after Ufer. He closed the door firmly behind Flynn and then proceeded up the stairway on his right, which led to the second-floor residence of Herman Rosenthal.

Rosenthal controlled virtually all the gambling in New York City and for the most part allowed it to run cleanly, since the odds usually favored the house anyway, and Herman Rosenthal was the house. Still, every now and then he liked to take a hand in the outcome of a fight or a race or, playing a game on a larger scale, a political election. In this case, it was the Morris-Flynn heavyweight fight scheduled for that Friday in October 1911.

When Kramer reached the upper hallway he went to the door of Rosenthal's office and knocked.

"Come in," a baritone voice called out.

Kramer opened the door, stepped in, shut the door behind him, and then stood virtually at attention.

"Did you see Ufer?" Rosenthal asked from behind his desk.

"Yes, sir."

"Is it fixed?"

"That's what he said, sir."

"Is that an opinion, Kramer?"

"No, sir, it wasn't meant to be."

Rosenthal stood up and approached Kramer. The contrast in size between the two was startling in that Kramer, at six foot six, stood exactly one foot taller than his employer, and weighed about a hundred pounds more.

Nevertheless, at five six and one hundred and fifty pounds, Rosenthal remained one of the "biggest" men in New York City.

He looked up at his right-hand man and said, "Come now, Kramer. You know you can speak your mind with me."

"Yes, sir. I don't trust Ufer, sir."

"You think he's dishonest?"

Kramer seemed to smirk—something that shocked Rosenthal until he convinced himself he was mistaken—and said, "That much goes without saying, sir, but that wasn't what I meant."

"What then?"

"He's weak."

Rosenthal smoothed his mustache with a thumbnail and said, "You can hardly blame the man for that, Kramer. We can't all be you."

"What I meant, sir, is that I don't think he was properly able to impress Flynn with the importance of this venture."

"I understand. You think that you should have accompanied Ufer when he spoke to Flynn?"

"Yes, sir."

"That decision was mine, Kramer," Rosenthal reminded his man. "I chose to exploit the man's greed and need for money, rather than utilize fear, which is your specialty."

"Yes, sir."

"It should work."

"I'm sure it will, sir."

"Don't 'yes, sir' me, Kramer," Rosenthal said, walking back to his desk. "That's not what I pay you for. If you don't agree with me, say so. I didn't hire you to be a goddamned yes-man."

"Yes, sir. It's not that I don't agree, sir," Kramer said, choosing his words carefully in order to avoid offending his boss. "I just think that my way would have worked . . . equally well, and possibly better."

"You just like to scare people, Kramer," Rosenthal said, seating himself behind his desk once again. "That's your problem."

"Yes, sir."

"But *I* scare *you,* don't I, Kramer?"

"Uh . . . yes, sir."

"So that's why we did it my way, isn't it?"

"That's right, sir."

"All right, Kramer. That'll be enough chitchat. Why don't you go downstairs in case we need someone to scare a customer who doesn't want to pay his bill?"

"As you wish, sir."

"Oh, and Kramer," Rosenthal said as his man was going out the door.

"Sir?"

"Try not to break anybody tonight? The last time it cost me plenty to keep you out of jail."

Kramer grimaced—a second unprecedented show of emotion in one night? —and replied, "Yes, sir."

Section One

The Fix

A good sport is a good loser who takes his medicine.

—Bat Masterson, June 18, 1911
The New York Morning Telegraph

CHAPTER ONE

The day Bat Masterson died on the backstretch of Belmont Park, William Barclay "Bat" Masterson was in the clubhouse watching.

"Christ," the two-legged Masterson said when he saw his four-legged namesake go down.

The jockey hit the dirt hard, but had the presence of mind to roll out of the way of the rest of the field and escape harm. The horse had been making a move on the outside, so the other horses and riders were able to avoid a pileup.

"Did you see what happened?" Inkspot Jones asked, nudging Bat with an elbow. "Did you see what made him fall?"

"He just fell, damn it!"

"He must have tripped over something."

"We'll have to wait to find out," Bat said. From his pocket he took five ten-dollar tickets and ripped them into little pieces.

"Don't rip 'em yet!" Inkspot cried in panic.

"You think that horse is gonna get up and beat the field to the finish line?" Bat demanded. "I've seen enough death in my lifetime to know what it looks like, Inkspot."

"He's dead?"

"He's deader than yesterday's news. Come on, let's get a drink."

Inkspot Jones stared in awe at the fallen horse for a few moments, as if willing it to get up, but when it didn't he shrugged, emulated his friend and tore up his tickets. It was the first time he had ever done that before the official results of a race.

Bat Masterson had been one of the greatest legends of the Old West, both as a gunman and as a gambler, but that was many years ago, in towns like Tombstone and Dodge City, when he was a young man. Not many of those legends made it into the twentieth century. His old compadre, Wyatt Earp, was somewhere in California, and he'd heard that old Bill Tilghman was still wearing a badge somewhere. He was past all that, though. Now he was Bat Masterson, a fifty-eight-year-old sportswriter for the *Morning Telegraph*, a prominent New York sporting journal, with his own column, "Bat Masterson's Views on Timely Topics," published every Tuesday, Thursday, and Saturday. Although he still carried his gun—old habits die the hardest, it's true—he had now added pen and typewriter to his personal arsenal, and he wielded them all with equal dexterity.

Inkspot Jones was also a writer for the *Telegraph,* and an old friend of Bat's from years before. It was Bat who had persuaded Inkspot to come to New York from Denver earlier that year, with his wife, and write for the *Morning Telegraph.*

Today was Monday, a breezy October day in 1911, and this was the day Bat and Inkspot always went to Belmont Park together to play the horses. They had watched Bat Masterson—the horse—run many times before, losing more than he won, but winning at nice prices when he did win, and today they had hoped would be one of those days.

Now those days were gone forever. Who would have expected the old nag to drop dead on the track?

It was almost like losing an old friend—and fifty dollars.

"Jesus," Bat said when they reached the bar, "when he loses, he really loses."

"What a shame."

Bat was dapper today—as usual—in a dark, three-piece suit, holding a flat-topped derby in one hand. Carrying around considerably more belly than he had in the days when he lived by his gun instead of his pen, he nevertheless cut an impressive figure, with his slicked-down dark hair sporting gray at the sides, and his carefully trimmed mustache. His wife of more than twenty-five years, the loyal, patient Emma, said that the older he got the handsomer he got . . . but then he lied to her, too.

Inkspot looked even more like an unmade bed than usual that day. His white hair was rumpled, his suit ill-fitting and dirty, mostly with cigarette ash and ink. It was the ever-present ink that had caused him to be nicknamed "Inkspot"—by Bat Masterson.

Over a couple of drinks Inkspot gave Bat a detailed explanation of the running of the next race, and why the three horse would win the next race.

"The five is the winner," Bat said, after his friend had run out of breath.

Inkspot took a deep breath, and Bat knew that he was about to go over his line of reasoning once again. He held up his hand to stop him and said, "You stick around and find out. I've had enough for today."

"But it's only the fifth race!"

"Four's plenty for me," Bat said, reaching into his pocket. "I'm just all broken up about the demise of my namesake."

"I'll pay for the drinks," Inkspot Jones said, uncharacteristically placing his hand over his friend's.

"You?" Bat asked, looking surprised. "You come into money of a sudden?"

"Not yet," Inkspot said, grinning enigmatically, "but soon."

Bat did not pursue the matter, but he felt sorry for his friend if he was going to bet big on the three horse in the next race, trying to get even. The only quicker way there was to lose money was to bet bigger trying to get *ahead.*

"Where are you off to, then?" Inkspot asked.

"I've got to go downtown to check out the Jim Flynn workout."

"Jim Flynn? What the hell does he have to work out for? He's a cinch."

"I know," Bat said, "I know he is." Then, unable to resist, he tapped the Racing Form in his friend's hand and added, "Just like the five horse in the next race."

"The three!" Inkspot insisted.

"You'll see," Bat said, tapping his friend's chest with his forefinger, "and *I'll* see *you* later."

Bat Masterson watched with interest as Jim Flynn worked out in the ring, sparring with another man. From what he could see, it could have been the other man who was training for a fight, and not Flynn.

Flynn appeared to be a singularly unspectacular, lumbering, slow, easy-to-hit heavyweight, and Bat Masterson knew that this wasn't the case. He had wondered why the Texan, Frank Ufer, had been taking as much Morris money as he could, bragging about his boy dethroning the black champion, Jack Johnson, after he finished The Pueblo Fireman. Bat knew what a workman Flynn was in the ring, but *this* Flynn who was now sparring in the ring did not remotely resemble *that* Flynn in the slightest, and maybe Ufer knew what he was doing.

Bat's nose twitched, offended by the distinct smell of a frame or a fix, and it wasn't only a result of what he was seeing in the ring. When he had arrived shortly before the sparring session, he had spotted Frank Ufer, Morris's manager, nearby. Now, while it wasn't unusual for the manager of the opposing fighter to watch the other fighter workout, there *was* something unusual about the kind of glance that had been exchanged by Ufer and Flynn. Bat's sharp eyes had caught the look, and it set his nose to twitching. What he saw in the ring now only intensified the stench of a fix.

Ufer and Bat were on opposite sides of the ring, and if one of the sparring fighters had passed between the glances *they* were throwing at each other, he would probably have been burned to a crisp.

Frank Ufer and Bat Masterson knew each other from Denver, where their feud had started and become almost legendary, and there was no love lost between them.

"What's the matter?" Damon Runyon asked him. "You look strange."

Bat had arranged to meet Runyon at the Forty-second Street Gym, just off Broadway, to watch The Pueblo Fireman work out. He enjoyed the company of the much younger man, and Runyon not only enjoyed being with Masterson, but felt he could learn a lot by listening to and observing the man, for whom he had a tremendous respect.

Alfred Damon Runyon had arrived in New York only months earlier and was covering the New York Giants baseball team for *The New York American*. An affinity had immediately formed between the two men when they first met, and the friendship had grown since then.

"I smell something," Bat replied.

Both men were standing at ringside, watching Flynn closely. Being members of the press, they were so permitted.

"So do I," Runyon said. "Sweaty socks and armpits. A stop at the Metropole will take care of that, though." The Metropole was one of Bat's favorite watering holes.

"That's not what I meant," Bat said, looking at his younger colleague, "but your idea is a sound one. What say we go and hoist a few?"

"You've seen enough?"

Bat grimaced and said, "I've seen more than enough."

Bat threw one more dirty look Frank Ufer's way, and then the two men left.

After Bat Masterson left the Forty-second Street Gym, Frank Ufer breathed a sigh of relief. He had been afraid that Masterson might sense something, and try to talk to Jim Flynn out of the fix.

That was silly, though. Why would Masterson suspect something? Ufer told himself that he was just paranoid about Masterson because of trouble they'd had with each other in Denver.

Ufer threw a glance Jim Flynn's way, then left to go supervise his own boy's workout.

On the way to the Metropole, which was located on Forty-second Street and Broadway only a few doors from the gym, Runyon asked, "How did you do at the track?"

"I died."

"I beg your pardon?"

"The nag that was named after me died."

"You mean, he folded in the stretch?" Runyon asked, still thinking that Bat was speaking in racing terms.

"I mean he died, damn it! He dropped dead on the backstretch."

"Oh," Runyon said. Then, "Oh! You mean he really died? The horse is dead?"

"Dead," Bat repeated, nodding. "As dead as this line of conversation. Let's talk about something else."

"Okay," Runyon agreed. "Let's talk about The Pueblo Fireman."

"Ha! What's to talk about? He ain't even breaking a sweat in the ring."

"What do you mean?"

"When you've refereed as many fights as I have, kid, you can smell a fix, and I smell a fix."

Another reason the thirty-one-year-old Runyon liked being with Masterson was the fact that the older man often referred to him as "kid" or "lad." When you pass thirty, you appreciate little things like that.

"But Flynn could take Morris easy."

"You've got a lot to learn, lad," Bat said as they ascended the front steps of the Metropole and entered. "Jim Flynn *should* beat Morris easily, but that don't necessarily mean that he will, or that he wants to. That's why it's called gambling. Doesn't the wrong team ever win in your sport?"

Runyon shrugged. "Baseball is baseball. There's not much you can do about that."

Bat shook his head and said, "Sure there is. You just have to buy off more than one person, that's all."

"You've got to have more than that to go on to suspect a fix, Bat."

"What more do you need than the presence of Frank Ufer?" Bat asked. "If Flynn was my fighter, I wouldn't let Ufer anywhere near him. The fact that he *was* there just makes the smell that much worse."

Damon Runyon opened his mouth to reply, then stopped as the enormity of Bat's words dawned on him.

George Considine, the owner of the Metropole Bar, spotted his friend Bat as soon as he and Runyon entered. Considine was the son of John Considine, a gambler from Seattle who had known Bat from the old days.

Lavishly furnished with ornate woodwork, small but elegant crystal chandeliers, and Rochester lamps, the Metropole Bar—housed within the famous Metropole Hotel—was a favorite gathering place not only of Bat Masterson and his friends but of major sports, theatrical, and gambling figures, as well as other members of the press.

"Table?" Considine asked.

"Bar," Bat said. "Let the paying, eating customers have the tables, George."

"Of course," Considine said. "Take the room away from the paying, drinking customers instead."

"George," Bat said patiently to his friend, "you know I pay my bills."

"Yes, you do," Considine agreed, then added, "eventually."

Bat took Runyon's arm and led him to the bar, away from the smiling Considine. "Listen," he said, "do you have any money on you?"

"Yes, why?"

"No reason," Bat said, patting the younger man on the back. "It's just a good idea always to have money on you. You never know when you'll run into an unexpected expense."

"Like a horse dying on the backstretch, you mean?" Runyon asked, grinning.

"Beer?" Bat asked him, ignoring the remark.

"That's fine."

Bat held up two fingers for the bartender to see, and the man nodded and brought over two mugs of beer. Bat looked around the place to see if he could spot any of his friends, but his crowd usually didn't show up at the Metropole until after dinner, and today was no different.

"So you really think there's a fix in the making?" Runyon asked after they had begun to slake their thirst.

"Shhh," Bat said, "not so loud, lad." He leaned closer to Runyon and said,

"There is the scent of one—actually, with Ufer being Morris's manager, I should say there's a definite stench!"

"Yes, but if there *is* a fix in the making," Runyon said in almost a whisper, "wouldn't Herman Rosenthal be involved, too?"

Runyon had been in New York only a few months, but already he knew enough to invoke Herman Rosenthal's name whenever something crooked popped up, especially if it involved gambling.

Bat wrinkled his nose and said, "Now we're moving onto words like 'stink'!"

"How are we going to find out for sure?" Runyon asked eagerly.

"We?"

"Well, now that we both know about it, we have to act on it, don't we?"

"Al," Bat said, one of the rare times he called the other man by his first name—his real first name. "We don't *know* a goddamned thing."

"We suspect—"

"*I* suspect," Bat corrected him before he could go any farther. "And if I *do* decide to do anything about it, I'll do it alone."

Runyon, looking hurt and chagrined, replied, "I was only offering my help."

"I understand that," Bat said, putting his hand on the younger man's shoulder in a conciliatory gesture, "and I appreciate it, but when I act on my hunches, I usually act alone."

"I understand."

"Some of my hunches have been known to be dangerous," Bat added, trying to soften the blow of refusing the younger man's offer of assistance.

"I'm not afraid."

Runyon's attitude was cocky, and Bat studied the younger man closely for a few moments, remembering when he was that age—was he *ever*—and felt the same way about danger.

"You'll have to learn to be," he told Alfred Damon Runyon.

Runyon didn't quite understand what that meant, but Bat declined to explain further. In time the younger man would find out for himself that sometimes it was smarter—and safer—to be afraid. Granted, he would probably learn the hard way, but then that was the best way to learn anything, because the lesson usually stuck.

"What are you gonna do, Bat?"

"The more I think about it, the surer I get that I'm right." Bat looked into his glass and said, "I think I'm gonna let the polecat out of the bag."

CHAPTER TWO

Early in 1903, when Bat Masterson was taking his journalistic first steps in Denver, the management of *The New York Morning Telegraph* changed hands.

Twenty years previous a cub reporter named William Eugene Lewis had listened intently to Bat Masterson's somewhat exaggerated tales of frontier life. Like his brother, Alfred Henry Lewis—who in 1905 penned *The Sunset Trail,* a novel loosely based on Bat Masterson's experiences in the West— William Eugene Lewis had followed Bat's career down through the years, and it was he who became managing editor of the *Telegraph* and asked Bat to come to New York and take a job as a reporter.

Now, some eight years later, Bat had a reputation for speaking his mind in his column, and this was what he did in the matter of the Flynn-Morris "fix."

The next morning he addressed the matter this way in his column: "There have been a good many cooked-up affairs pulled off in the prize-ring, but hardly one quite as daring, or that smells so much like a polecat, as the one between Jim Flynn and Carl Morris. Throw in the presence of Morris's manager, Frank Ufer, and the smell becomes downright offensive!"

Frank Ufer's reaction was immediate. He agreed to give an interview in *The New York Globe,* in which he ripped into Bat Masterson, claiming that the "legend" had built up a phony reputation by shooting innocent cowboys in the back.

Many of Bat's colleagues—including Damon Runyon—were quite surprised by Bat's reaction to the affront.

"I can't believe how calm you are," Damon Runyon said the morning following the appearance of the *Globe* interview. They were in the city room of the Telegraph Building, which was located at Eighth Avenue and Fiftieth Street.

"A cool head has kept me alive for many years, lad," Bat replied, "but don't think that I'm taking it lightly."

So saying, Bat rose from his desk preparatory to leaving the office.

"What are you gonna do?" Runyon asked as Bat walked past him. "Where are you going?"

"To talk to the horse's mouth," Bat threw back over his shoulder.

He was going to talk directly to Jim Flynn.

Bat Masterson's conversation with The Pueblo Fireman was short and to the point. He found the fighter at the Forty-second Street Gym alone, but had no idea how much time he would have with Flynn before his manager showed up, so he got right to the point.

"How much are you getting to throw this Morris fight, Jim?"

Flustered and unable to look Masterson in the eye and lie to him, Flynn blurted, "Seventy-five hundred dollars!"

Shaking his head sadly, Bat said, "You're a fool!" He left the fighter and went directly back to his desk at the *Morning Telegraph*.

His column the following day, and every day up until the fight, relentlessly belabored the point of the fight fix.

Finally the day of the fight arrived, and if Bat's column and Ufer's interview accomplished nothing else, they probably swelled the size of the gate by a significant margin.

The fight was scheduled to go off in Madison Square Garden, New York's palace of sports events. Initially located in an abandoned railroad warehouse at Madison Square, on Madison Avenue and East Twenty-sixth Street, in 1874, the Garden was later rebuilt on the same site in 1890, to the specifications of architect Stanford White, and had become the mecca of sports events in New York—especially boxing. It was the mark of a significant bout for a fight to be held in the Garden, and this was where the Flynn-Morris fight was to be fought.

When Frank Ufer arrived at the Garden for the fight, he was met at the East Twenty-sixth Street entrance by a street urchin bearing a brown-paper-wrapped package, bound with brown cord.

"Mr. Ufer?"

Ufer frowned at the filthy lad and said, "What do you want?"

"I got something for you," the kid said, holding the package out to him.

"What is it?" the fight manager asked, accepting it by reflex.

"I don't know," the boy said. "A man give me two bits to wait here for you and give it to you." And so saying, the lad turned and ran off eagerly to spend his fortune.

Ufer, unable to contain his curiosity about the contents of the small package, tore it open on the spot and felt a cold chill down his back. Inside the package was the packet of bills—the seventy-five hundred dollars—that he had paid Jim Flynn to throw the fight.

"Damn him!" Ufer said.

Of course, he was not referring to The Pueblo Fireman, but to Bat Masterson. He was sure that it was Masterson's infernal column that had caused the fighter to renege on their deal and return the money.

Ufer hurriedly stuffed the bills out of sight in his jacket pocket and then studied his hands, which were shaking. When Flynn knocked out his man, Morris—as he knew he would—Herman Rosenthal was not going to be happy, and it wouldn't do any good to blame Bat Masterson. It wouldn't matter to Rosenthal that Masterson's column had caused Flynn to go back on their deal. Rosenthal would hold *Ufer* responsible, because it was Ufer who was supposed to have seen to it that the deal *did* go off without a hitch.

All Ufer could do was go inside and pray for a miracle. Morris was a huge man. Maybe he would get lucky and land a blow flush on The Pueblo Fireman's chin. If that didn't happen—and Ufer, ever the gambler, would not have taken money on it—then all that would be left for Ufer to do was disappear before Rosenthal—or, he thought shuddering, his man Kramer—could find him.

Damn Bat Masterson to hell! If there was way in heaven or hell for him to get even, by God—or the Devil—he would!

Jim Flynn handed Carl Morris a terrific beating that night. Bat Masterson had successfully sniffed out and thwarted the fixing of an important fight.

Bat wasn't finished with Frank Ufer, however. He brought suit against the Texas millionaire and *The New York Globe* for defamation of character, even though Ufer had left New York to avoid Herman Rosenthal. Ufer still planned to have his revenge against Bat Masterson, but his thirst for it was tempered by his fear of Rosenthal.

Revenge would come later—after he made sure he stayed alive long enough to achieve it.

Early the morning after the fight Lou Kramer entered Herman Rosenthal's office and approached the crime kingpin's desk.

"Flynn won," Kramer said, "and Ufer's gone."

Rosenthal stared impassively at Kramer for a few moments before he spoke. "Masterson."

"His columns got to Flynn, I guess."

"Ufer has millions," Rosenthal said, "and what did he pay Flynn?"

"Seventy-five hundred."

Rosenthal laughed, a humorless explosion of sound that Kramer had heard only once or twice before.

"Should we look for him?"

"Be realistic, Kramer," Rosenthal said. "Ufer's got millions of dollars to hide behind."

"What do we do, then?"

"We wait for him to feel safe," Rosenthal said. "He'll show up someplace, sooner or later."

"And what about Masterson?"

"What about him?" Rosenthal asked. "You want to kill a living legend? That would really bring the heat down on us—especially Lieutenant Becker."

Charles Becker was a New York City police lieutenant who worked both sides of the fence. In some things he even went so far as to think of himself as Herman Rosenthal's partner. Rosenthal's problem was that Becker was also a friend of Bat Masterson's. That kind of situation had to be handled carefully, and correctly.

"You mean we're not going to do anything?" Kramer asked, looking puzzled.

"We're going to wait, Kramer," Rosenthal said. "Didn't you ever hear about all things coming to those that wait? Well, Frank Ufer and Bat Masterson will get everything that's coming to them." A hard look came over Rosenthal's face, and he added, "Just put the word out on the street that I'm not happy. Mr. Masterson's a little past his prime. Maybe we can make him sweat a bit."

"Right, boss."

Kramer, never one to second-guess his boss in his presence, turned to leave the room, but was stopped at the door by Rosenthal's voice.

"Kramer?"

"Yes, sir?"

"Don't you want to tell me something?"

Kramer frowned and turned to face his boss. "What's that, sir?"

"Don't you want to tell me 'I told you so'?"

"No, sir."

Rosenthal caught Kramer's eyes and held them, and the big man's eyes never flinched. Once again, Rosenthal congratulated himself on choosing his right-hand man well. Kramer was strong, stubborn, and smart—smart enough to know who the boss was.

"What about that other matter?"

"The newspaperman?"

"Yes."

"I'm afraid he's being troublesome, Mr. Rosenthal."

"Just troublesome?"

"Well, stubborn might be a better word. I just don't think he's going to back down on this thing."

"And why should he?" Rosenthal said. "From his point of view he stands to make a lot of money out of this."

"Yes, sir."

"All right, we can afford to give him some more time to come around to our way of thinking, Kramer."

"How much more?"

"I'll tell you when the time is up."

"And then what?"

"Well," Rosenthal said, "he's not anywhere near being a living legend, is he?"

"No, sir."

Kramer waited patiently for Rosenthal's final word on the matter, and when it came he was glad to see that he might finally have something to do.

"You'll kill him."

Lou Kramer left Herman Rosenthal's office, above the Fourteenth Street restaurant, and then left the building to make his way to 104 West Forty-fifth Street, where the biggest of Rosenthal's gambling establishments was located. It was his job to make sure that things were going smoothly there, and in all of Rosenthal's other businesses.

Kramer decided to walk, undaunted by the darkness and possible dangers of a late-night stroll in the big city. Lou Kramer felt confident that he could handle anything that came his way.

He wasn't really afraid of Herman Rosenthal, although he let the man think he was. What he was, though, was mindful of the fact that it was Rosenthal's brain that kept *his* pockets full of money, and he didn't want to take a chance of ruining that. He'd do whatever the man wanted him to do, as long as he paid him.

Although the massive Kramer could have broken Rosenthal's back with ease, he had never even entertained thoughts of usurping Rosenthal from the throne of his crime empire, because he knew his limitations. He just wasn't smart enough to do the things that Herman Rosenthal could do.

Then again, he could take solace in the fact that the diminutive crime kingpin could never do the things that he could do.

They made a good team.

CHAPTER THREE

Just as Bat Masterson's favorite watering hole was the Metropole Bar, his favorite restaurant was Shanley's Grill, a popular steakhouse at Broadway and Forty-third Street. Shanley's was somewhat less ostentatious than the Metropole Bar. As far as Bat was concerned, the Metropole was for drinking, and Shanley's was for eating. On almost any evening he could be found there at dinnertime, hunched over a thick steak. Bat had never been the kind of man who could relax at home over a nice quiet dinner with his wife, and Emma understood that. He didn't quite know how she had put up with him all these years, but he thanked the Lord that she had.

He was in Shanley's Grill the evening after the fight, eating dinner alone, when Lieutenant Charles Becker entered.

Lieutenant Becker's position made it relatively easy for him to turn certain situations to his own advantage, and he regularly did so. A case in point was when Herman Rosenthal needed a loan of fifteen hundred dollars to begin his gambling establishment on Forty-fifth Street, the one that served as the springboard to his present position as one of New York's premier crime bosses —along with Big Jack Zelig, Italian gang leader Paul Kelly, and street-gang leader Monk Eastman. It was Becker who had loaned Rosenthal the money, effectively getting in on the ground floor of Rosenthal's empire—and he had been squeezing the man ever since. He sometimes justified his actions by reasoning that by being Rosenthal's silent partner, he was putting a crimp into the businesses of Zelig, Kelly, and Eastman.

One of the people who had fallen under the spell of Bat Masterson's past happened to be Charles Becker, who at first had been somewhat in awe of Bat, and later found himself being accepted as a friend.

It was in his capacity, then, as Bat's friend that he sought him out and found him in his customary place at Shanley's Grill.

Normally, Bat Masterson was unable to enjoy a quiet dinner at Shanley's because of the number of people who simply wanted to be in his presence and hear stories of the Old West, but on this particular evening Becker found him sitting alone, enjoying his steak and seltzer lemonade.

"Sit down, Charles," Bat invited. "Have a seltzer lemonade."

Becker sat, but refused the lemonade, making a face. He was a man in his late thirties, tall and slender, with an angular face and intense gray eyes.

"I can't see how you can drink that stuff."

"Didn't have it out west, Charles," Bat said. "It's just a preamble to my drinking at the Metropole later on. What can I do for you this evening?"

"You can watch your ass, for one thing." Becker waved away a waiter who had been moving toward the table.

"Would you like to make that a little clearer?"

"You blew the fix on the Flynn-Morris fight last night, Bat."

"You knew about that?" Bat asked, popping a piece of steak into his mouth.

"I know about it now," Becker said carefully. "Certain people are not too happy about it."

"Are we talking about Herman Rosenthal?"

"Rosenthal, Zelig, Kelly, what's the difference? Somebody's mad, and somebody could decide to take it out on you."

"The only person I know who might be mad at me is my bookie, Charles, but I've paid him off. Even if I hadn't, he wouldn't be mad enough to hurt me."

"I'm not talking about hurting you."

Bat put down his knife and fork and looked across the table at the younger man. "We're playing word games here, Charles. You're saying Rosenthal might decide to have me killed. I say he's not that dumb. Killing me would draw too much attention to him and the others. Hell, if he killed me, Zelig and Kelly wouldn't like it."

"All I'm saying is watch your back, Bat."

"I've been doing that for more years than you've been alive, Charles," Bat said, picking up his knife and fork again, "but I appreciate the advice. All right?"

"All right," Becker said, understanding that Bat had just called a halt to that particular conversation.

"You want to hang around while I finish this and then take a walk with me over to the Metropole?"

"I don't think your friends would welcome me with open arms, Bat," Becker said, rising. "Besides, I've got business to take care of."

"All right, then," Bat said, looking up at the tall, lanky policeman. "Take some of your own advice, will you?"

"What's that?"

"Watch your back—from an old lawman to a young one, eh?"

"Sure," Becker said, grinning at the older man with some affection. "See you, Bat."

Bat watched the retreating back of Lieutenant Charles Becker, and had no doubt but that the man was on his way to see Mr. Herman Rosenthal.

Unless he'd gone there first.

Lieutenant Becker had *not* gone to see Rosenthal before seeing Bat Masterson, but he did go to Fourteenth Street immediately upon leaving Shanley's Grill.

He was met at the door of the restaurant by Kramer, who took him up to Rosenthal's office, without any conversation passing between the two. To say that the two men didn't like each other was an understatement.

"Ah, Charles," Rosenthal said from behind his desk, "come in, sit down."

"No need for me to sit down, Herman," Becker said, moving into the center of the room.

Kramer closed the office door and took up a position just inside of it.

"I only came to give you a piece of advice."

"And what would that be?"

"I wouldn't want to see anything happen to Bat Masterson."

"Is that advice?" Rosenthal asked. "It sounds more like—"

"Let's just say that the word on the street has it that someone is upset about the outcome of the fight last night," Becker said, interrupting the other man. "That wouldn't be you, would it?"

"I may have lost a few dollars on the fight, Charles but why would that have anything to do with Bat Masterson?"

"I'm sure you read his column, Herman," Becker said, and then, paraphrasing Masterson's words to him earlier, he said, "Let's not play word games. The fix was supposed to be in last night, but Masterson's column changed that. I don't want anything to happen to him because of it."

"Well, neither do I. That wouldn't be good business, Charles."

"No, it wouldn't. I'm glad you realize that, Herman."

"Of course I realize it, Charles. I always know what's good for my business."

"All right. Now that we've got that settled, I might as well collect my cut tonight."

"A day early, aren't you?"

Becker shrugged and said, "I'm here."

"So you are," Rosenthal said. He opened his middle drawer and drew out a brown envelope. Becker came forward and accepted the proffered envelope, tucking it away without inspecting the contents. Rosenthal hadn't short changed him yet.

Becker turned and walked to the door, where Kramer stood with his back against it. The two men stared at each other coldly, until finally Kramer moved away from the door and opened it.

"Kramer won't bother to walk you out, Charles."

"Best news I've had all day," Becker said, and left.

Kramer shut the door behind him.

"You should let me kill him," Kramer said after Becker was gone. "You should have let me kill him a long time ago."

"You just don't like him, Kramer, but he is useful to us."

"And when he stops being useful?"

"Then" he'll be killed, and maybe I'll even let you do it."

Kramer grinned tightly and said, "Best news I've had all day."

After finishing his dinner at Shanley's Grill, Bat walked one block south to the Metropole, where he found his friends already gathered, swapping lies.

On his way to join his friends Bat nodded greetings to Irwin S. Cobb, a rewrite man for the *Morning World;* Diamond Jim Brady, who also owned his own café and bar not far from where they were now on Broadway; Rube Marquard, the New York Giants' left-handed pitcher, who after two medio-cre years had won twenty-four games and led the league in strikeouts; and Nat Fleischer, possibly the foremost authority on boxing in the world, and the only man Bat would admit knew more about the pugilistic arts than he did.

Being the sports enthusiast that he was, Bat stopped to shake hands and have a few words with Fleischer, and with Marquard, whom he had met only a few weeks before, introduced by Damon Runyon.

With Christy Mathewson, Marquard had formed a formidable righty-lefty combination that had produced fifty victories and led the Giants to a first-place finish in the National League, even though in April they had lost their home park, the Polo Grounds, to a fire that had forced them to share High-lander Park with the American League's sixth-place New York Yankees. Back on top after failing to win in 1910, John McGraw's Giants were beaten by Connie Mack's Philadelphia A's four games to two, due in part to the hitting of the A's third baseman, Frank Baker. After hitting a home run to beat the Giants two days in a row, Baker became known as "Home Run" Baker.

Still, Marquard's performance boded will for the Giants' future seasons. Bat told the pitcher that he was sure the Giants would win the World Series next year, and continued on.

When Bat reached his friends' table, the circle of whopper-swapping friends who were there included:

Tom O'Rourke, a fight promoter who had known Bat since the days of John L. Sullivan's reign as heavyweight champ;

William Muldoon, another promoter and old friend of Bat's, who would later become boxing commissioner of New York;

Val O'Farrell, a detective on the New York City police force;

Finley Peter Dunne, general manager of the *Morning Telegraph*, Bat's paper;

and Damon Runyon, who was easily the youngest man present.

"There he is," Val O'Farrell announced as Bat approached their table, "the savior of boxing in New York." O'Farrell was a man in his forties who was almost dapper enough to rival Bat. He was also acknowledged as the best detective on the force.

They all applauded Bat as he grinned and took a seat at the table.

"Hey, George!" Fin Dunne called out to George Considine. "The conquering hero is here. Bring him a drink." Dunne was in his fifties, but could easily have passed for sixty. Thirty hard years in the newspaper business had done that to him, but had not dimmed his sense of humor. He hadn't changed his wardrobe much either. He was still wearing the same suits he had worn years before, disdaining the newer fashions sported by men like Val O'Farrell and Bat Masterson. He was an old *war*horse, he liked to tell people, not a *clothes*horse.

Considine obliged, playing waiter if only to try to persuade the group to keep the racket down—at least until he could satisfy his customers and join them.

"Here's your drink, Bat," Considine said, putting a huge mug of beer in front of him. "Now see what you can do about keeping your rowdy friends quieted down."

"You know I'll do my best, George," Bat promised, "but you know what my chances are with this group."

Considine shook his head and went back to placate his paying customers.

"Tell us how you did it, Bat," invited Tom O'Rourke, who *was* sixty and looked it. "How'd you sniff out that big bad fix?" Tom was another man who wore the newer fashions, but he preferred loud clothes, as his brightly checked jacket attested.

Bat looked around at the faces regarding him and noticed somebody missing. "Anybody seen Inkspot?" Bat asked. "I haven't seen him since we were at the track Monday."

"He's been acting real strange of late," Bill Muldoon said. The promoter was Bat's age, but while Bat had grown thicker with age, Muldoon had grown leaner and, as a result, looked somewhat regal in stature, in the manner of Abraham Lincoln.

"I noticed that," O'Rourke said. "He keeps hinting that he's going to be coming into a lot of money soon."

"He told me that at the track," Bat said, "but I thought he was talking about hitting it big on a horse."

"Did he?"

"Not that day," Bat said, recalling that the five horse had lost in the fifth race—as had the three horse that Bat had picked, upholding his decision to leave the track when he did. "I don't get it, then." Bat looked at his friends. "What's he playing at?"

"Maybe we should find him and ask," Damon Runyon suggested.

"I don't think so," Bat said. "If he wanted us to know, he'd have told someone by now."

"Someone like you," Dunne said. "It's no secret that he has little use for any of us."

"And vice versa, right?"

"That's not fair—" Dunne began.

"Come on, Will. Inkspot just isn't your type, is he? Or any of you, for that matter. You don't like the way he dresses, the way he acts—"

"He is rather hard to get to know," Muldoon said, "or like, but you don't hold that against us, do you, Bat?"

"Of course not."

"You've been friends with him a long time."

"A long time, yes, but that doesn't mean I expect all of you to be."

"So you mean to tell us that he hasn't told you what he's up to?" Dunne asked.

"Not a peep. We'll just have to wait to find out until he's good and ready."

"What about you, Bat?" O'Rourke asked.

"What about me?"

"You ready to regale us with the story of how you sniffed out that fix?"

"Well," Bat said, wrapping both hands around his beer mug, "if you all insist . . ."

Two weeks after Bat Masterson last saw Delaney "Inkspot" Jones at Belmont Park, his wife, Ida, reported him missing to the New York City Police Department.

When asked why she hadn't reported him missing earlier, Mrs. Jones said, "Jones told me that he was working on something real important that was going to make us a lot of money, and that I shouldn't worry if he was gone for a few days at a time."

When asked why she had decided to report him now, she answered, "He didn't say anything about weeks."

Section Two

Bat Masterson, Investigator

This is the biggest boob town in America.

—Bat Masterson, September 29, 1921
The New York Morning Telegraph

CHAPTER FOUR

New York
December 1911

The first week of December 1911 was cold and rainy. Inkspot Jones was still missing, and Bat Masterson was promoted to vice-president of the *Morning Telegraph*.

The vice-presidency really didn't mean all that much to Bat, except for a little more freedom as to what he wrote, and when. He maintained the Tuesday, Thursday, and Saturday schedule of his column, "Masterson's Views on Timely Topics," but on occasion took a flyer out of the area of sports and dropped in an opinion on the state of the world, as he viewed it.

Like the inability of the New York City Police Department to find a missing person.

Damon Runyon, with the baseball season over, had also turned his attention to other things and, although he did not have a regular column of his own in which to make his opinions known, he did an occasional byline piece on the effectiveness—or ineffectiveness—of the police in finding the missing newspaperman, Inkspot Jones.

Runyon wrote: "We are a close group, newsmen, in that when one of our number is in trouble, we would all like to help. If anyone knows the whereabouts of Delaney Jones, I wish they would get in touch with me at the offices of the New York American."

As a result of Runyon's piece in the *American*, Bat invited him to lunch and allowed the younger man to pick the place. They met at Runyon's favorite lunchtime restaurant, a place called Dowling's, farther north on Broadway than Shanley's. As far as what kind of place Dowling's was, suffice to say that Dowling's was to Shanley's what Shanley's was to the Metropole Bar.

Bat ordered a tongue sandwich and a seltzer lemonade, while Damon Runyon had his usual, two five-cent beers and snacks from the free-lunch counter.

"You should eat more than that," Bat said.

"I do," Runyon replied, "for dinner."

Damon Runyon usually started his day with a five-cent beer for breakfast at a dive called Coddington's. He then hit Dowling's for lunch, stopped somewhere in the late afternoon for a snack at Frank Geraghty's—usually salami—and then for dinner he'd stop at Mack's and have pickles, herring, hard-boiled eggs, and beer.

"I've seen your dinners." Bat made a face, and then he turned the conversation to other things. "Wish I had thought of putting a message like that in my column, Al."

When Alfred Damon Runyon had arrived in New York and started his job on the *American*, he handed in his first piece to the sports editor, Harry Cashman, who took one look at that three-name byline and changed it.

"Don't like it," Cashman had said, "so from now on you'll be Damon Runyon."

Runyon still liked his friends to call him Al—which, after all, was what he had been called for over thirty years—even though he thoroughly liked his new byline.

"I appreciate that, Bat," he said now.

"You're taking a chance, though."

"What do you mean?"

"Well, did it ever occur to you that Inkspot's not missing of his own accord?"

"You mean, somebody arranged it?"

Bat nodded and bit into his tongue sandwich. "And that somebody may not want you to be putting your nose in where it don't belong," he said, chewing. "Don't you have some sports event that you could cover out of town or something?"

"Baseball's my sport, Bat."

"And it ain't baseball season."

"I know," Runyon said, "so Harry Cashman arranged for me to do that piece."

"You should have told me the idea and let me do it," Bat said. "They won't come gunning for me the way they might for you."

"Gunning for me?" Runyon looked faintly amused. "This isn't Dodge City, Bat."

"I know that. I ain't senile, but we've got varmints in New York, too, kid. All I'm saying is that I'm better equipped to handle them than you are."

"I'm not leaving New York, Bat," Runyon said stubbornly. "Not until the Giants' first road trip anyway."

Which, they both knew, wouldn't be until April of the following year.

"Then from now until that time, my friend," Bat said, "or until this all blows over, I'm your shadow."

"That's not practical, Bat—" Runyon began, but before he could make his point, both men spotted Lieutenant Charles Becker advancing toward their table.

"I've been looking for you, Runyon."

"You found me."

Runyon didn't like Charles Becker, and made no attempt to hide the fact. The feeling was quite mutual.

"What the hell do you mean by this?" Becker demanded, slamming down a copy of that morning's *American* on the table. Bat noticed that it was folded over to reveal Runyon's article.

"Just what it says, Lieutenant," Runyon replied. "I figure the police need a little help, and I intend to give it to them."

"We don't need your help, Runyon."

"Now, Charlie—" Bat began, but Becker spun on him angrily, cutting him off.

"Don't you get into this, Bat," he said. "I been catching hell from Commissioner Cropsey about you and your columns because he knows you're a friend of mine, but if you don't let up on me about this Jones business . . ."

James C. Cropsey had been the personal choice of Mayor William J. Gaynor and, although he was a fairly forceful man, he was not known to be especially competent.

"Let up on you?" Bat asked, frowning. "My columns are about the police in general, Charlie. I ain't made mention of you at all."

"And how long is that gonna last?" Becker asked. Addressing both men, he said, "The police don't need any help from the press, so you fellas better find yourselves something else to write about."

With that, Becker turned on his heels and angrily stalked out of Dowling's, leaving some surprised customers behind who buzzed among themselves for the next few minutes, casting glances over at Bat Masterson and Damon Runyon.

"Speaking of varmints," Runyon said, "how can you be friends with a man like that?"

Bat glanced at Runyon and said, "Don't ever question a man's choice of friends, Mr. Runyon. That's for a man to do himself."

"Sorry."

"Just don't get him mad at you."

"Are *you* going to take what he said to heart?"

"I'm going to think on it," Bat said, finishing off his sandwich.

"Well, think about something else while you're at it, will you?"

"What?"

"You spent your share of years upholding the law out west, Bat."

"My brother Ed was more a lawman than I was."

"That's hogwash, but I don't want to argue that."

"What *do* you want to argue, then?"

"Nothing. I want you to think about looking for Inkspot Jones ourselves."

Bat peered at Runyon carefully and said, *"Ourselves?"*

"Well, you'll do most of the detective work, but I'll be along to help."

"I ain't no detective."

"You're friends with the Pinkertons, aren't you?"

"Now you sound like my wife, Runyon," Bat said irritably. "I *know* Will Pinkerton, yes, but that doesn't mean—"

"And you've got experience as a lawman. Why, as recently as 1905 you were a deputy U.S. marshal."

"I'm impressed with your knowledge of my past, but those days are over."

"Inkspot's your friend, isn't he?"

"He is," Bat said, standing up, "and I want him found, but I ain't the one to do it, believe me."

"Well, somebody should."

Bat brushed crumbs from his suit and asked, "You going back to your office?"

"Yes."

"All right." Bat stood up and put on his overcoat. "I've got some things to take care of, but I'll meet you at your office. Don't leave until I get there. Remember, you and me are joined at the hip from now until Inkspot is found."

Runyon grinned at Bat's retreating back and said, "I wouldn't have it any other way."

The rain of the past few days had finally let up. During the walk to his office on Eighth Avenue, Bat thought back to a conversation he'd had with his wife that morning, very much like the one he'd just had with Damon Runyon. . . .

"I've been talking to Delaney Jones's wife," Emma had said at breakfast. "Poor Ida."

Knowing full well what kind of a man he was, that once he left his home in the morning he probably wouldn't return until after Emma had gone to sleep, Bat tried to at least have a cup of coffee with her each morning.

"How is she holding up?"

"Bat," Emma Masterson said, very carefully, "she wants you to try and find Inkspot."

"What are you talking about?"

"Ida says the police aren't doing very well finding him," she went on quickly, as if she wanted to get the words out as fast as she could. "She feels that since you're his best friend, and you were a lawman, that you could probably find him."

"The trail's pretty cold by now," he said. "Besides, did you tell her that I'm a newspaperman, not a detective?"

"I, uh—"

Bat frowned and looked at his wife, who was aging well, if not gracefully. The best that could be said for her was that she looked her age—a few years younger than himself—and wore it pleasantly.

"Emma?" Bat was trying to be patient. "You didn't encourage this nonsense, did you?"

"I told her I'd talk to you about it."

"Emma—" His tone plainly indicated that his patience was waning.

"Well, you could try, couldn't you?"

"No, I couldn't, Emma. I haven't worn a badge in years—"

"The last time was—"

"—and I was *never* a detective."

"You're friends with the Pinkertons, you must have worked with them."

Bat blew air out of his mouth in a gesture of helplessness. "Emma, whose side are you on?"

"Ida is so dismayed, Bat. She's worried that Inkspot might be dead."

"Dead? He's probably on a bender somewhere, maybe because he hit it big at the track."

"Did he?"

"How do I know?" Bat stood up. "I have to go to work, Emma."

"Bat, you've been writing all those columns about the police not being able to find Inkspot," she said, walking to the door with him. "Don't tell me that you don't think you could do a better job than they're doing?"

Bat stared at his wife of twenty-five years and said, "Don't try to con a con man, Emma."

"I'm sorry," she said, looking properly chastised, "but I feel so sorry for her." She started to button his coat for him and added, "I can just imagine how I would feel if you were missing."

That stopped him, and his expression softened as he studied his wife's face. "Emma . . ."

"Yes?"

He kissed her softly on the cheek and said, "I'll think about it."

But he hadn't really, because he had gotten busy, and then had to meet Runyon for lunch.

So he thought about it now.

Everyone—well, Emma and Al Runyon—seemed to think that he would have some sort of leg up on the police in finding Inkspot Jones, because of his past, and because he and Inkspot were friends.

Of course he was worried about Inkspot, but he'd known men to hit it big at the track and take off before, leaving behind their wives and their jobs . . . only Inkspot didn't strike him as that kind of a man. What he'd said about Inkspot's being out on a bender had been just plain dumb. Inkspot liked his whiskey, but he wasn't the type to get drunk for days on end, leaving his wife to worry.

No, Inkspot had been gone too long, even for a gambler, and maybe somebody who cared *should* be the one to try to find him, instead of somebody—Becker, or whoever was assigned—who was just doing his job.

Still, there was Becker's threat if Bat interfered, so if he did intend to "investigate," he was going to need some sort of official status to produce for the police if things got tough, to keep him out of trouble.

And, of course, as Emma and Runyon had so eloquently pointed out, he *was* friends with William Pinkerton.

After running a few errands, Bat went to the offices of the *American* and found Runyon seated at his desk working on something.

"Bat," Runyon said, frowning at the piece of paper he had in his typewriter, "I'll be with you in a minute."

Bat waited patiently while Runyon finished what he was writing. Writing? He was *typing*. Bat wrote in longhand, couldn't even bring himself to try one of those typewriters. There were just certain pieces of the twentieth century —typewriters, elevators, automobiles—that Bat couldn't quite bring himself to accept. And yet they were a big part of New York, and he loved New York.

Go make sense out of that.

Runyon finished what he was doing and then looked up at him. "You know, this business of being my nursemaid isn't really necessary Bat," he started, but Bat cut him off before he could go any farther.

"Talk to your editor, Al," he said. "You're gonna need some time off."

"For what?"

"You win," Bat said, spreading his hands as if surrendering. "I'm a detective."

CHAPTER FIVE

The first stop the next day for the newly formed detective team of Masterson and Runyon was Inkspot Jones's desk at the offices of the *Morning Telegraph*. They went through it in the presence of Managing Editor William E. Lewis.

"What was he working on, Will?" Bat asked as he sat at the desk and started opening drawers.

"He was covering the races, boxing, baseball when the season was in," Lewis said with a shrug.

"Was he sticking his nose into the crime beat at all?" Runyon asked while Bat was shuffling through some papers he had brought out and put on the desk.

"No, definitely not."

"You mean you didn't assign him to any crime stories, don't you?"

"Well, of course, why would I? He's a sports reporter, not a damn crime reporter."

"There's nothing that says he couldn't have been working on something on his own, right?" This time Bat looked up at Will Lewis.

"Well now, I wouldn't know that, would I, Bat?"

"No," Bat said, dumping the papers back into the drawer and opening another one, "but somebody must know."

"If I didn't," Lewis said, "and you didn't, Bat, then who would?"

"His wife," Runyon said, picking his butt up off the corner of Inkspot Jones's desk. "I could go and talk to her, Bat."

"We'll go together, kid," Bat said, "as soon as we're finished here."

"Bat, I've got work to do . . ." Lewis said.

"You can go, Will, as long as you're satisfied that I'm not taking anything that doesn't belong to me."

"You?" Lewis said, snorting. "Take anything you need that might help you find him, Bat. If he's out on a bender, though, know this."

"What?"

"He's fired."

"I'll tell him." Bat closed the drawer and opened a third one.

"Want me to look at something?" Runyon offered.

"No, it wouldn't help. I know Inkspot, I know how he thinks. There might be something here that would get past you, but it won't get by me."

"What am I along for, then?"

Bat looked at Runyon and said, "This was your idea, lad, for me to play detective—although it wasn't a very original one."

On the way to the Telegraph Building Bat had told Runyon about the conversation he'd had with his wife.

"Your wife doesn't know that you've agreed yet, does she? That you've decided to go ahead and investigate?"

"No."

"When will you tell her?"

"I'll tell her tonight," Bat said, still shuffling papers, stopping to read a line here, a paragraph there, "or in the morning." Telling her would be admitting that she was right and he was wrong, and *that* could be done in time. "Look, why don't you talk to some of the fellas up here, see if Inkspot said anything to them."

"If he didn't tell you, what makes you think he'd tell anyone else?"

"Maybe it slipped out," Bat said. "Go on, I need some time to go through this mess."

If Bat had emptied the drawers out on Inkspot's desk top it couldn't have looked worse than it already did. The man's desk looked like he dressed.

Most of the papers in the desk were copies of old stories, some of them months old, some only days old. The earliest ones went back to the Polo Grounds fire, and the most recent to the death of a horse named Bat Masterson on the backstretch at Belmont Park.

When Runyon returned from talking to some of the other reporters, Bat was sitting quietly in Inkspot's chair, staring off into space.

"Anything?"

Bat looked up and said, "What did the others say?"

"Nobody knows anything. Inkspot let something slip once or twice about coming into money, but he never said when, or how."

Bat waved a finger at Runyon. "He made a remark like that to me at the track, but I thought he was talking about hitting it big on a horse."

"Then if it wasn't that, what was it?"

Bat shook his head, pulling at his bottom lip and said, "I don't know. I wish I'd pressed him that day, but I thought he was talking about a damned horse."

A few moments of silence went by, and then Runyon asked, "Did you find anything in his desk?"

"I don't know," Bat said, tapping the desk lightly with his fist. "I don't know. . . ."

Runyon didn't know if Bat was answering his question, or even if he'd heard him. He was about to repeat himself when Bat stood up.

"All right," he said, picking up his flat-topped derby. "Let's go and talk to Mrs. Inkspot Jones."

Delaney and Ida Jones had rooms at the Essex Hotel, located at the corner of Madison Avenue and Fifty-sixth Street. It wasn't one of the more expensive hotels in New York, but it was far from the bottom of the barrel.

"Inkspot must have saved his money," Runyon said.

Bat didn't say anything. He'd been there only one other time since Inkspot had arrived in New York, and he'd had the same exact thought. He had never pursued it, just as he hadn't pushed his friend that last day at the track, when he'd made the remark about coming into money. You don't push your friends, Bat Masterson always thought.

Maybe he should change his way of thinking.

"I'd never keep a room here," Runyon said as they entered the place.

"Why not?"

"Too far from Times Square and Broadway."

"Well, Inkspot wasn't the Broadway rat that we are, young Runyon."

"What did he do with his off time?"

"If I knew that I'd know more about why he's missing, wouldn't I?"

In the elevator Runyon said, "I thought you were friends."

"That doesn't mean we were joined at the hip, does it? *We're* friends and I don't know what *you* do when *you're* relaxing." Bat's tone was defensive.

"The same thing I do when I'm not," Runyon said, "just like you."

"Yeah."

As the elevator jerked to a stop, Bat looked up and said, "I can't get used to these damn things."

"Why ride them, then?"

"The old legs ain't what they used to be." With that, Bat stepped from the elevator and led the way down the hall.

Though he had been to Inkspot's apartment only once before, he remembered the room number. When he reached it, he knocked on the door as Runyon caught up to him.

"Old legs," Runyon said sarcastically.

The door opened, and a small, dark-haired wisp of a woman appeared. She looked up at Bat with tired, bloodshot eyes and then extended her hands to him.

"William," she said, drawing a look from Runyon. He'd never heard anyone call Bat by his real name before.

"Hello, Ida."

"Come in," she said, and then, seeing Runyon, added, "you and your friend, come in, please."

Bat allowed her to draw him into the apartment and Runyon followed, closing the door behind him.

"Ida, this is my friend and colleague, Damon Runyon."

Ida looked past Bat and said, "I've heard my husband speak of you, Mr. Runyon. He says you have a God-given talent for writing."

"That's very kind, Mrs. Jones." Runyon reacted awkwardly to the praise.

"Please, call me Ida."

"And I hope you will call me Al."

"Thank you," she said, and then directed her attention back to Bat, whose hands she was still holding. "Bat, are you here for the reason I think?"

"I guess I am, Ida."

"When Emma said that you might do this for us, I didn't dare hope—"

"Ida, we have to talk seriously."

"Of course." She finally released his hands, and Bat seized the opportunity to remove his hat. "Let me take your coats. Please, sit down."

There was a divan and a love seat, and Bat chose to sit on the divan, Runyon following suit and sitting next to him.

"Shall I get some coffee, or tea?" she asked. "Perhaps something stronger?"

"No, nothing," Bat said, answering for both himself and Runyon. "Sit down with us, Ida."

"Very well," she said, and sat down, laying her hands in her lap, where they fluttered like wounded birds. She was unable to keep them still.

"Ida, you have to know from the outset that I am not a detective."

"I don't care about that, Bat," she said, falling back on his more familiar name. "You were a lawman, and you are my husband's friend. If anyone can find him, it's you."

"That's very flattering, Ida. I'm going to do my best, and young Runyon here is going to help me."

"We have some questions we'd like to ask you, Ida," Runyon said, jumping in on cue.

"Anything."

"Ida, did you notice a change in Inkspot over the past few months?"

"Yes, I did. He was nervous at times, and at other times he seemed—I don't know how to describe it."

"Excited about something?" Bat asked, prompting her.

"Yes, extremely excited, but holding it in somehow."

"And when did this start?"

"I'd say more than two months ago."

"A significant amount of time before he . . . disappeared?" Runyon asked.

"Y-yes."

"Did he ever say what he was nervous or excited about?"

"No," she said, shaking her head. "I asked him once or twice, but he just told me not to worry, that everything would work out. I—I often had the feeling that it involved . . . money, somehow."

"A lot of money?" Bat asked.

"It must have been," Ida Jones replied. "Only a great sum of money could get my husband that worked up."

"Do you have any idea what he might have been doing to result in his coming into a great sum of money?"

"No, I don't. I've thought and I've thought, but I can't come up—"

"All right, Ida, all right," Bat said soothingly as she began to get worked up herself. "Just relax."

"All right," she said, staring down into her lap and examining her fluttering hands.

"Ida, did—does Inkspot talk to you about his assignments? His stories?"

"No. He knows I don't like sports, so he rarely talks about his business at home."

This wasn't getting them anywhere, Bat realized, but at least knowing that he was looking for Inkspot might put Ida Jones's mind to rest to a small degree.

It certainly wasn't doing anything to still her nervous hands.

Bat and Runyon took their leave, Bat assuring Ida that he would keep in touch with her, either himself or through his wife.

"I can't tell you how much this means to me, William," Ida said at the door, and then she embarrassed Bat by kissing his right hand.

Bat and Runyon rode down in the elevator in silence, neither one of them speaking until they'd reached the street.

"What did we find out?" Runyon asked.

"Just what we knew, that Inkspot was going to come into some money. We still don't know when, or how."

"She's a nice lady."

"Yes, she is. You feel like a walk?"

"Sure."

That was just one other thing the two men had in common. Neither of them ever minded a walk on the streets of New York. Bat had spent most of his life in western towns, but when he finally reached New York—via Denver —he felt as if he had truly come home.

As for Damon Runyon, he was born in Manhattan, Kansas, and much preferred Manhattan, New York.

CHAPTER SIX

True to the "Broadway rats" name that Bat had hung on them, Bat and Runyon walked through a light drizzle to the Metropole on Broadway and Forty-second Street and installed themselves at the bar.

"One drink," Bat said as they entered, "and then we're off to Shanley's for dinner."

"Shanley's? I thought we'd eat at Mack's."

Bat made a face.

"What kind of partnership is this going to be if we keep eating at your places?" Runyon insisted.

In fairness Bat said, "All right, don't get testy. Tonight Shanley's, tomorrow Mack's. Agreed?"

"Agreed."

They shared one drink at the Metropole, told George Considine they'd return after dinner, and then went to Shanley's for dinner, each ordering his usual.

"Let's talk about the practicality of this business of your being my shadow until baseball season, Bat."

"All right, so it's a little impractical," Bat agreed. "Let's just say I'll do my best to keep you alive until certain people get over your column."

"And you alive until certain people get over a fight that didn't stay fixed."

"Down the hatch," Bat said, lifting his beer mug to toast both of them staying alive, a toast that Runyon agreed with heartily.

"We didn't find out very much today, Bat," Runyon said, picking a hard-boiled egg off his plate.

"I told you I wasn't a damned detective."

"I'm not blaming you," Runyon was quick to add. "We did what we could, there just wasn't anything there to find out. What are we going to do tomorrow?"

"I don't know. Are you going back home to Flushing tonight?"

Runyon lived with his wife in a boardinghouse in Flushing, Queens.

"No. I have access room at the Gotham Hotel for nights when I don't want to make the trip home."

"Well, that's good. I'd hate to have you turn up dead between here and Flushing."

"Bat, I don't think I can really take this business seriously—I mean, about my life being in danger."

"Suit yourself," Bat said with a shrug. "I ain't gonna argue with you about it."

"You still haven't said what we're going to be doing tomorrow."

"That's because I still don't know what we're gonna do tomorrow, if anything."

"Bat, we can't quit on this after only one day."

"Where else is there to look, kid? I was hoping that Inkspot's desk or his wife would be able to tell us something, but that didn't pan out. What's next?"

Runyon nibbled on a herring and regarded Bat balefully across the table.

"All right," Bat said suddenly, "get that look out of your eyes. By morning I'll have come up with something. We're not giving up."

"That's great," Runyon said, and happily stuffed the herring into his mouth.

Bat made a face and put his hand against his stomach.

Half an hour later they left Shanley's to walk back to the Metropole, which was actually closer to half a block away rather than a full block. Still, a lot can happen in half a block in New York.

And often did.

They were only about ten feet from the entrance of Shanley's when Bat suddenly shouted, "Look out!" and shoved the younger man away from him.

Runyon went sprawling. When he'd righted himself and looked up, what a sight Bat Masterson was to behold. There was the legendary Mr. Masterson, fifty-eight if he was a day, holding his own while slugging it out with three street thugs. From his vantage point Runyon could see that Bat's gray eyes were glittering, and the look on his face one of pure enjoyment. In that moment Runyon believed all of the stories he'd ever heard about Bat Masterson, but he also knew that it wouldn't be long before Bat ran out of steam, and it was time for him to get up off his ass and help.

He got to his feet and, with a mighty yell, ran toward the four men as fast as he could, barreling into Bat's assailants with all his might. He brought two of them to the wet ground with him, rolling with them, kicking and punching to beat the band, *getting* just a tad more than he was giving.

Suddenly one man was lifted off of him and sent sprawling, and the other simply got up on his own and ran off, following his two colleagues.

"By God, what a fight," Bat said, reaching down and hauling Runyon to his feet. "You all right, lad?"

"Fine," Runyon said, gasping for breath. He studied Bat's face for signs of damage, spotted a knot on his forehead and a small cut on his left eyebrow. Other than that, he didn't look much the worse for wear.

"Don't be looking at me like that," Bat said, grinning. "You should see *your* face."

Runyon put his hands to his face and then walked the ten feet back to Shanley's to use the glass door as a mirror. He had a strawberry scrape high on his right cheek, and his bottom lip was cut.

"Not too bad," he said, touching the back of his hand to his lip and walking back to Bat, who was vainly trying to brush filth and wetness from his overcoat.

"You'll live," Bat said. "We both will. Nothing like a little scrap to keep your heart pumping."

Bat was blustering, but Runyon could see that the older man was still trying to catch his breath, while he himself was already beginning to breathe easier.

"Bat, maybe we should get you—get ourselves to a doctor, huh?"

"Nonsense," Bat said, looking down at the ground. "Where's my hat—ah, there it is." He bent over to retrieve his hat and said, "Not even damaged," before once again addressing himself to Runyon's suggestion. "We don't need any damned sawbones, kid. We've got to get over to the Metropole."

"Like this? Wet and beat up?"

"Well, of course like this. You think that pack would believe our story if we cleaned up first? Come on!"

Shaking his head, Runyon hurried to keep up with Bat, who although still huffing and puffing some, was setting a fierce pace.

"Don't you carry a gun?" Runyon asked, coming abreast of him.

"A gun? As you pointed out to me earlier today, my friend, this is not Dodge City."

"I know, but—"

"Besides, we didn't need a gun to take care of those three. We did fine."

"Were they thieves, do you think, Bat?"

"After our wallets? Maybe," Bat said, and then added, "and then again maybe you had better think again about the consequences of what you wrote in that article, Mr. Runyon."

It started to rain again.

While Bat Masterson and Damon Runyon were telling lies to their friends about the ten thugs they had whipped with their fists, in the back room of a Five Points restaurant on Mulberry Street, there was a meeting taking place. Three men were seated at a round table, and against three of the four walls of the room, three other men were leaning.

Around the year 1820 the Five Points section of Manhattan got its name from five streets—Little Water, Cross, Anthony, Orange, and Mulberry—all of which bordered an area of about an acre. Eventually, the routes of the five streets changed, and so did their names, but the area remained known as Five Points.

Numerous gangs sprang up from Five Points, most notably the Chinchesters, Roach Guards. Plug Uglies, Shirt Tails, and Dead Rabbits.

The Roach Guards were named after a Five Points liquor dealer. The

Dead Rabbits broke off from this group when, during an angry gang meeting, a dead rabbit was hurled into the middle of the floor. The Shirt Tail gang was so named because their members wore their shirts outside their pants. The Plug Uglies were named after the oversized plug hats they wore. The hats were stuffed with leather and wool and, during gang battles, the hats were pulled down over their ears. In this manner they served as helmets.

Over the years the gangs became organized and, in time, became an effective weapon in politics, sometimes influencing elections through brute force.

Eventually the gangs melded into two separate, warring factions, the control of which passed from hand to hand as time went by.

At the present time, the Five Pointers, successors to the Dead Rabbits, Plug Uglies and other gangs, ruled the area between Broadway and the Bowery, Fourteenth Street and City Hall Park. They had several hundred members, and were run by a man named Paolo Antonini Vaccarelli, more commonly called Paul Kelly. Kelly owned the New Brighton Dance Hall on Great Jones Street and Third Avenue, where the gang usually held their meetings.

The Eastmans, the rival gang, which also had several hundred members, took their name from their present leader, Monk Eastman and controlled the area from Monroe Street to Fourteenth Street, from the Bowery to the East River. They met in a dive on Chrystie Street, off the Bowery.

Two of the men at the Mulberry Street meetings were Paul Kelly and Monk Eastman.

The third man was looked upon as an interloper in their midst.

His name was Herman Rosenthal.

Neither Kelly nor Eastman liked Rosenthal—hell, they didn't like each other, but at least *they* came from the streets of New York. They didn't know where Rosenthal hailed from, but it sure as hell wasn't New York.

Mulberry Street presented neutral ground for the three crime leaders.

"Let's get this over with," Rosenthal said. "I have business to attend to."

"We all do, Rosenthal," Paul Kelly said. "That's why we're here." Kelly was a nondescript man of average height, soft-spoken and conservatively dressed. He looked more like a businessman than a gang leader.

"Well, you fellas called this meeting," Rosenthal said to Kelly and Eastman. "What's on your minds?"

Eastman was the opposite of Paul Kelly. Monk *looked* like a gangster, with a bullet-shaped head set on a short bull neck. His face was covered with knife scars from fights in his past, while Kelly—who had been a bantamweight boxer for a time—did not take part in common street fights, but bore certain marks on his face from his ring days.

"*You're* on our minds, Rosenthal," Eastman said.

Behind Rosenthal, leaning against the wall, stood Kramer, alert and ready. Likewise, the other two men had brought their "Kramers," each of whom reclined against the wall behind his leader.

"We have heard that you are upset because your fight fix did not go off as planned," Kelly said. He was a self-educated man who tried to present a somewhat cultural front, despite his street ancestry.

"We all have business deals that go awry, gentlemen," Rosenthal said, spreading his hands. "Is that all you asked me here to discuss?"

"We know that Bat Masterson is the one who blew your fix, Rosenthal," Eastman said, "and we don't need for something to happen to a man like that. It would bring too much attention down on all of us."

"Herman," Paul Kelly said, "don't kill Bat Masterson. That's what we're here to tell you."

"Is that a fact?" Rosenthal asked. "You brought me here to tell me how to conduct my business? You think you have that right?"

"When your business effects our business, yeah, we got that right," Eastman said.

"We are merely making a suggestion," Kelly said, "in the hopes that you will take it."

"A suggestion," Rosenthal repeated thoughtfully. "You both must know that the problem with the fight fix was a minor one. Why would I have Masterson killed for that?"

"You telling us that you won't?" Eastman asked. "That you didn't put the word out on him?"

"I'm not telling you anything," Rosenthal said. "I don't ask you about your business, and you shouldn't be asking me about mine." With that, he rose and said, "I'm leaving. Please don't ask for a meeting again unless you have something truly important to discuss . . . gentlemen."

Rosenthal moved toward the door, which Kramer opened for him, and then left with Kramer backing out behind him.

"I tell you what we should do," Eastman said. "We should have *him* taken out of the way."

"That would have the same result as killing a man like Bat Masterson," Paul Kelly said. "No, I have the feeling that Mr. 'Uptown' Rosenthal will bring about his own end without our help, sooner or later, especially if he continues to play with fire."

"You mean Becker?"

"I mean Becker."

"Becker's lightweight."

"*Bantam*weight, maybe," Kelly said with a wistful smile, "but bantams can sting, too."

Kelly and Eastman regarded each other for a moment, and then Eastman said, "Well, I hope Rosenthal gets his soon. It's bad enough sharing New York with you without having him around, too."

Neither man commented on the presence in New York of Big Jack Zelig. He was in a class all by himself.

In a taxi on their way back to Fourteenth Street, Kramer said to Rosenthal, "You should have let me take care of them."

"Kramer, Kramer," Rosenthal said, shaking his head, "that's all you want to do to people is take care of them. When will you learn that there are other ways?"

"They shouldn't have talked to you like that," Kramer said. "They shouldn't try and tell you how to run your business."

"Well now, you've got that right," Rosenthal said approvingly. "Don't worry, my friend, soon enough Kelly and Eastman will be gone, and then we will have control over it all."

Kramer thought that Rosenthal was talking to him almost as if they were partners.

Sure, Kramer knew he wasn't smart enough himself to run it all, but all of a sudden a *partnership* didn't sound too bad.

CHAPTER SEVEN

When Bat woke the following morning, his muscles ached from the fight and his head from the lies and drinking that took place afterward. He vaguely remembered accompanying Damon Runyon to the Gotham Hotel, but could not remember dragging himself home.

Pushing himself up to a seated position—slowly, and not without some pain—he wondered if Emma had been awake when he arrived home, and if she knew what had happened.

"You're up, are you?" Mrs. Masterson asked as she entered the room carrying a tray.

"Barely."

"Let me prop up your pillows," she said, laying the tray at the foot of the bed. To his annoyance she fluffed up two pillows behind him and helped him lean back against them like some old man.

Setting the tray on his lap then, she said, "This is what you get for brawling in the streets and not coming straight home afterward. Teach you to go to the Metropole and brag instead of coming home to rest. Does it hurt?"

"Of course it hurts, woman."

"Well, thank the Lord you don't feel you have to lie to *me*."

"When have I ever lied to you?" Bat surveyed the food on the tray: eggs, bacon, fresh biscuits, and coffee.

"We shall not go into that now," she said. "Eat your breakfast."

"To what do I owe this feast?" he asked, staring down at the marvelous breakfast, which he had absolutely no desire to eat.

"When you came home last night you were staggering around so much, bumping into furniture, that you woke me."

"I'm sorry."

"I'm not," she said. "While I was readying you for bed you told me what you and young Damon Runyon did. I'm sure Ida was comforted by your visit, Bat."

"I hope she was," he said, nibbling at a piece of toast and suddenly discovering an appetite. "I don't know how much good we're going to do her, though."

"You'll try," Emma Masterson said. "That's all you can do, and I'm grateful for that, William."

"Stop yapping at me and let me eat my breakfast, woman," he said gruffly, but Mrs. Masterson was not to be fooled. She leaned over, kissed her husband on the forehead fondly, and left him to his morning meal.

And aches and pains.

Mr. Damon Runyon, being younger—and not having drunk as much, nor taken as many blows—had a considerably easier morning than Mr. Bat Masterson. Runyon didn't know if Bat would remember that they had agreed to meet at Coddington's, on Seventh Avenue and Fifty-first Street, but he repaired to that place in any case and sat with his five-cent beer breakfast, waiting for his partner in detection.

He hoped that Bat would have figured out what their next move should be, but doubted that the older man would be in shape to do anything but fall down.

"How can you drink that so early?" Bat Masterson said. He appeared in front of Runyon's table and was regarding him with puzzlement and disgust.

"It's what I have for breakfast," Runyon said, sipping again. He frowned at Bat and said, "To tell you the truth, I didn't expect you to show up."

"Sorry I'm late." Bat lowered himself gingerly into the chair across the table from Runyon. "Emma chose this morning to make me a complete breakfast."

"She knows, then?"

"I can't recall telling her," Bat confessed, "but yes, she knows, and she quite approves."

"Did you have the, uh, time to figure out what our next move should be?"

"I may have gotten knocked around a bit, and drank a bit, but my brains aren't addled, man."

"Then you have?"

"I have."

"What are we going to do, then?"

"You are going to finish your . . . breakfast," Bat said, barely containing his disgust, "and then we are going to the races, my friend."

"The races?"

Bat nodded. "Belmont Park, to be exact."

"For God's sake—"

"Inkspot spent—spends a lot of his time at that track, lad, and it just might be that someone there knows more than we do."

"Well," Runyon said, putting his mug down and standing up, "that won't be hard."

When Bat didn't move, Runyon asked, "Are you coming?"

"We've got time, Al," Bat said, pushing himself carefully to his feet, "we've got time."

Belmont Park wasn't fifty years old yet, but it was closing in fast. The best horses in the world, the best jockeys and trainers came there to ply their trades, but it was winter now, and there was no racing. All the horses and their connections had headed for warmer climates, like Florida or California. Still, there was a skeleton crew of people at Belmont, some of whom might have known Inkspot Jones, and have some idea where he was.

Bat and Runyon bypassed the empty grandstand and clubhouse and went directly to the area of the stables, where some trainers kept their horses all year round. It was owners, trainers, and the other track workers—exercise riders, hotwalkers—that Bat wanted to talk to, because at one time or another most of them should have spoken to Inkspot, in his capacity either as a reporter or as a horse player.

The trip, however, proved futile, for no one had any idea where Inkspot might be, and none of them had heard the newspaperman say how or when he might be coming into a lot of money.

"Believe them all?" Runyon asked Bat in the taxi back to the city.

"Why would any of them lie?"

"We're dealing with a crime here."

"Are we?"

"Don't you think so? Or do you think he's gone on his own?"

"I don't know. I'm starting to be sorry I got involved in this, only I'm too worried about him to quit looking."

"Where else do we look?"

"That's something else I'm worried about."

They stopped at the Metropole, and as soon as they entered, Bat spotted Charles Becker.

"Uh-oh."

"What?" It was a second or two before Runyon, too, spotted the police lieutenant. "Uh-oh."

"Go to the bar, kid. Let me talk to him."

Runyon went to the bar, and George Considine approached Bat.

"How long's he been here, George?"

"Came in looking for you. He's been here about an hour, and he's not very good for business, Bat. Can you get him out of here?"

"Give us a table, George. The faster I talk to him, the faster he'll leave."

"All right."

Becker came up to them then, and Bat spoke before the policeman could. "George is going to give us a table, Charles. We can talk there."

"Good, because we've got plenty to talk about." Becker was scowling.

The policeman seemed barely able to contain himself until they were seated, and then he exploded. "What the hell do you think you're trying to do?"

"You want to explain that?"

"You're asking questions, Bat, about Inkspot Jones. I told you not to get involved."

"And I didn't want to, Charles, but you've got to admit that the police haven't had much luck looking for him. I just figured that maybe somebody who knew him would have a better chance."

"And have you?"

"No."

"Because you don't know what you're doing. You're not a detective, Bat."

"I was a lawman for enough years—"

"That was a long time ago."

"Not so long."

"And you got yourself beat up, didn't you?"

"Where'd you hear that?"

"You must be kidding. Everybody in this place knows about it."

"I handled myself all right."

"You and that guy Runyon. You getting him involved, too?"

"He's just helping me out, Charles."

"I could lock you up, Bat—the both of you—you know that."

Bat ignored the remark. He didn't want to play his hole card just yet. "What's your problem, Charles?"

"I'm getting heat from my boss."

"Cropsey?"

"Who else is my boss?"

"Where's *he* getting heat from?"

"I can't tell you that."

"Can't?"

"I don't know."

Bat knew of Becker's relationship with Herman Rosenthal, and he knew of Herman Rosenthal's relationship with Big Tim Sullivan, a state senator and, some said, gambling czar. Could Sullivan have been the one putting pressure on the police commissioner? On behalf of Rosenthal? Did it then follow that Rosenthal had something to do with Inkspot's disappearance? It was Bat that Rosenthal was mad at after the fight fix went awry. He would have more reason to get rid of Bat than he would Inkspot, wouldn't he? Unless Inkspot knew something really big . . .

"What's going on, Charles?" Bat asked, frowning. "Do you know something about Inkspot's disappearance?"

"I don't know anything, Bat."

"Well, tell me what you *feel*, then."

Becker paused a moment, then gave Bat a look and said, "You want to know what I think? I think he's dead."

"Dead? Why?"

"Because nobody disappears that good, without a trace like that. We've got people who are trained to find people who are missing, or who don't want to be found, and they can't find a trail. What do you expect to do?"

"Maybe I expect to care whether he's found or not, alive or not," Bat explained. "Your trained people couldn't give a good damn less. To them it's just a job—or is it more than that to you?"

"The fact that it's my job is enough, Bat." Becker stood up. "You should have learned something from what happened last night."

"What happened last night?" Bat asked innocently. "A couple of thugs tried to steal my wallet."

"You're not dumb enough to think that, Bat, but while you're trying to convince yourself, remember one thing. You're my friend, but you've got no official standing. If you get in my way, I'll lock you up."

"Don't try it, Charles. You'll wind up with egg on your face."

"What are you talking about?"

Bat decided to play his ace in the hole after all. He reached into his pocket and pulled out a telegram, one he'd received from William Pinkerton in Chicago.

"Here," he said, handing it over, "read this."

The telegram said that Bat Masterson was a representative of the Pinkerton Detective Agency, and was acting on their behalf in the matter of the disappearance of New York newspaperman Delaney Jones.

"You've got no license." Becker handed the telegram back. "You've got no official standing."

"It's on the way, Charles," Bat said, tucking the telegram away. "As far as anyone is concerned, I'm a licensed Pinkerton detective. You can't lock me up for minding Pinkerton's business."

"Smart move, Bat," Becker said, shaking his head, "but you might have just smart-moved yourself into an early grave."

"Charles, when you've led a life like I have and you've managed to reach my age, your early-grave days are far behind you."

"Now, what was that about?" Damon Runyon asked, joining Bat with two beers after Lieutenant Becker had left.

Bat looked at the beer Runyon had brought him and took it, taking two healthy swallows.

"He doesn't want me getting in his way," Bat replied, but it was obvious that his mind was only half on his answer.

"And?"

Bat took the Pinkerton telegram out again and passed it to Runyon, who read it.

"You didn't tell me about this." Runyon put it down on the table, and his tone said he was slightly hurt.

"Son," Bat said, picking it up again, "you never tell anybody about your ace in the hole unless you have to."

"So why now?"

"To get Becker off my back, and to keep you from wondering what I did to accomplish that."

"Like paying him off?"

"Like paying him off."

Runyon thought it over a moment and then said, "All right, that's fair."

Bat nodded, tucked away the telegram again, and picked up his beer.

"What about me?"

"What about you?"

"What's my standing in all this?"

"You're helping me, that's all. If things get too hot, you can just walk away."

"I wouldn't."

"I know that. All I'm saying is that you could."

Runyon realized that if anything were to go wrong, Bat Masterson would be the one taking all the blame and all the chances—and he'd set it up that way himself.

"Well, what did you find out from Becker?"

Bat scowled and said, "Now, that's what's bothering me. It's not so much what he *did* tell me as what he *didn't.*"

"For instance?"

"Cropsey's getting some pressure."

"The police commissioner?"

"Right," Bat said, looking as if he was trying to reason this out. "Now, who's big enough to put pressure on the police commissioner but a politician?"

"Like who?" Runyon was playing his part of sounding board.

"Like Big Tim Sullivan."

"But isn't Sullivan a supporter of Rosenthal?"

"That he is."

"What would Herman Rosenthal have to do with Inkspot Jones? They sure don't travel in the same circles."

"Well, maybe that's what we ought to try and find out next."

"Now, wait a minute, Bat. You're talking about going to see Rosenthal or at least nosing around in his affairs."

"That's what I'm talking about, I guess."

"That's unhealthy talk. You're not exactly high on Rosenthal's list of friends—or have you forgotten about the fight?"

"No, I haven't forgotten about the fight, but you're the one who wanted me to get into this—you and my wife. You want me to pull out now because things might get rough? She wouldn't, I can tell you that."

"Maybe she would if you told her that you were going to have to see Rosenthal."

Bat stared across the table at Runyon and said, "Why don't you let me worry about that?"

"I've got an idea."

"What?"

"Why don't you let me go and see Rosenthal? He probably doesn't even know who I am."

"What would you tell him?"

"That I was looking for Inkspot Jones. The worst he can do is tell me he doesn't know what I'm talking about, but maybe he'll let something slip. Who knows?"

"Who knows?" Bat repeated. He had to admit that the idea had merit. If he went to see Rosenthal himself, he'd be tempting the man to take some action against him. If young Runyon went to see him, maybe all he'd do was have Kramer throw him out. More than likely, whether he knew something about Inkspot's disappearance or not, he'd just lie to Runyon and that would be the end of it.

Runyon continued to plead his case. "I'm a newspaperman looking for another newspaperman. What would be so odd about that?"

"Nothing," Bat said, "nothing at all—as long as you're sure you want to do this."

"I'm sure."

"You don't want to think it over?"

"No . . . if I do that, I might change my mind."

Bat's face brightened, and he looked at Runyon the way a proud father would look at a son, saying, "By God, Al, you're learning."

They decided that the meeting between Runyon and Rosenthal would not take place until the following day. Runyon told Bat that he wouldn't be going back to Flushing tonight either, but would be staying at the Gotham again. They had dinner at Mack's—after Runyon reminded Bat of their agreement —then returned to the Metropole, where they found that most of their cohorts obviously had something else to do that night. They took the opportunity to do less drinking and more talking, specifically to discuss just how Damon Runyon would approach his meeting with Herman Rosenthal—starting with the fact that it would be in broad daylight.

CHAPTER EIGHT

Damon Runyon arrived at Herman Rosenthal's Fourteenth Street restaurant, at Union Square, for breakfast. After he'd finished eating a somewhat more conventional breakfast than he was used to, he called the waiter over.

"Yes, sir?"

"Is Mr. Rosenthal around?"

The waiter looked nervous enough that Runyon assumed that no one ever *asked* to see Rosenthal willingly.

"Uh, I'd have to check, sir. Was there . . . something you didn't like?"

"No, no," Runyon replied, wondering if *that* was really what the waiter was worried about, that his boss would get a complaint about him. "I just want to talk to him about a mutual . . . acquaintance."

"Uh, I'll check, sir."

"And let me have some more coffee while I'm waiting, will you?"

"Of course."

The waiter poured him another cup and then went away, supposedly to do his checking.

Sipping his coffee, Runyon went over in his mind everything Bat had told him. It had been fascinating to him to listen to Bat, because he felt that it gave him some insight into what the older man must have been like years ago.

"Watch his eyes," Bat had said. "I don't care if it's Kramer or Rosenthal, watch his eyes, because if something is going to happen, you'll see it there first.

"And whatever you do, don't let them know that you're nervous . . ."

Runyon hadn't bothered to deny that he'd be nervous. He dried his palms on his pants so that his coffee cup wouldn't slip out of his hands and took another sip. He would rather have had a five-cent beer.

He looked in the direction the waiter had gone and suddenly the man reappeared, followed a scant second later by a huge man walking behind him. According to Bat's description, this was Lou Kramer.

Runyon made a concerted effort not to dry his palms again and reached for his cup, but it slid from his grasp and spilled its remains onto the tablecloth.

"That's all right, sir," the waiter said, rushing over to start cleaning it. "I'll take care of that. This," the man said, casting a sidelong glance at Kramer, as if he were afraid to look right at him, "is Mr. Rosenthal's assistant, Mr. Kramer."

"Oh, well," Runyon said, getting to his feet, "I really wanted to see Mr. Rosenthal himself."

"What do you want to talk to Mr. Rosenthal about?" Kramer asked, staring down at Runyon from his superior height.

"Uh, about a mutual acquaintance."

"You said that," Kramer said, cutting him off. "Who?"

"Oh, who?" Runyon said. "Well, uh, Mr. Rosenthal probably knows him as Delaney Jones, or Inkspot Jones."

Kramer's eyes narrowed as he stared at Damon Runyon, and then said gruffly, "Follow me."

Runyon picked up his coat and followed Kramer to a stairway at the front of the store that he had noticed when he entered, and then up the stairs to the next floor and a large oak door. Kramer knocked and entered without waiting for a reply.

Runyon followed him into the room and immediately became aware of the man behind the desk. He was a much smaller man than Kramer, yet his presence dominated the room.

Herman Rosenthal, of course.

"Mr. Rosenthal?"

"That's right," Rosenthal said, casting a glance at Kramer. Runyon did not look at Kramer to see if he was giving some sort of silent reply. He preferred to keep his eyes on Rosenthal.

"Mr. Kramer seems to feel that you might have something to say that would be of some interest to me." Rosenthal's tone said plainly that he doubted as much. "Is that true?"

"I might. I hope I do."

"Say it, then, and we can both judge."

"I'm looking for Inkspot Jones."

Rosenthal did not reply.

"Inkspot Jones?" Runyon repeated.

Rosenthal regarded Runyon in silence for a few seconds before speaking. "Why do you come to me about it?"

"Inkspot Jones is a newsman who disappeared some time ago—"

"I read the newspapers, Mr. Runyon."

Rosenthal's use of his name shocked him a bit, because he had not introduced himself to either of the three men he'd spoken to in the restaurant—the waiter, Kramer, and finally Rosenthal—and yet the crime boss had addressed him by name. It made him feel as if something was crawling on his skin.

"I'd still like to know why you're coming to me about it." Rosenthal said again.

"I've been looking for him, and someone told me that you might know something about his disappearance."

Runyon expected to be asked who had given him that information, but instead Rosenthal began to laugh.

"You're being very evasive, Mr. Runyon, so let me help you," Rosenthal said magnanimously. "You're here on behalf of our mutual . . . acquaintance, Bat Masterson. Now, why Mr. Masterson thinks that I would know anything about his friend's disappearance is something I cannot understand, but since he did not see fit to come here himself, you can tell him that he's wrong."

Damon Runyon was stumped. He wasn't quite sure how to handle the situation.

"I see you were unprepared for this," Rosenthal said. "Let me help you further. Tell Mr. Masterson I know nothing about his friend Jones's disappearance. Tell him also that I applaud his attempts to locate the man, but that I would appreciate his keeping clear of me while he's looking. That's all. Mr. Kramer will show you out."

Runyon looked at Kramer, who had already opened the door. As he walked toward it, Rosenthal suddenly spoke again.

"Mr. Runyon?"

"Yes?"

"I enjoy your columns very much."

Runyon waited to see if there was more, but when there was nothing he left, and followed Kramer downstairs, where the big man showed him the door.

"I haven't paid for my meal," Runyon said.

"It's on the house," Kramer said, and closed the door in his face.

Bat was at this desk finishing a column when Runyon reached the Morning Telegraph Building.

"How did it go?" he asked.

"I need a drink."

"That bad?"

"Worse."

Bat opened the bottom drawer of his desk and took out a bottle of whiskey and a coffee cup. He poured in a drop or two and passed it to Runyon, who propped his hip on the desk.

"What happened?"

Runyon swallowed a drop, made a face, and said, "He knew who I was. He knew that I was there for you. He knows all about us, Bat."

"Does that surprise you?" Bat asked. "The man has eyes and ears all over the city, Al. That's the reason he is where he is."

"Well, I tell you, I felt like somebody had been sleeping in my bed," Runyon said. He drank the rest of the whiskey, made a bigger face than before, and put the cup down.

"More?"

"Jesus, no. Are you done here?"

"Yep."

"Let's go someplace."

As they were leaving the building, Bat asked, "What else did he say?"

Runyon related everything Rosenthal had told him, word for word.

"Nothing about the fight?"

"No, just about Inkspot. *Does* he know anything, Bat, do you think?"

"If he didn't, he wouldn't have talked to you. I'm sure of that."

"Then he knows where Inkspot is."

Bat rubbed his jaw as they reached the street and asked, "Where do you want to go?"

"Someplace for a beer."

Rather than walk to the Metropole, they stopped into the nearest place, a hole in the wall called Billy's. They stood at the bar and ordered a beer each.

"What about it?" Runyon asked.

"I can't believe that Rosenthal would just put Inkspot somewhere and hold him there."

"What would he have to do with Inkspot in the first place?"

"See how this strikes you. Inkspot finds out something that could really hurt Rosenthal, and he decides to turn it into money."

"The money he'd been hinting that he was going to come into!"

"Right."

"You know Inkspot better than I do, Bat. Would he do that?"

Bat had to think about it. "Maybe he'd already been doing it in a small way," he finally said.

"The suite at the Essex House?"

Bat nodded. "Maybe he decided to go for a bigger chunk of money, get it all at once."

"Wouldn't his wife know about that?"

"I don't know," Bat said. "I'm just talking, Al, but if any of this is true, then he's not the Inkspot I knew before he came to New York. If that's the case, then I can't say what he would or wouldn't do."

"What about Rosenthal? Would he pay Inkspot?"

"Rosenthal would do whatever was most convenient for him. If it was convenient to pay Inkspot small sums of money from time to time, he'd do it. After all, a newspaperman might be of some use to him. If it stopped being convenient . . ."

"He'd kill him?"

Bat nodded.

"Is that what you think happened?"

Bat stared into his beer, swirled it around a little, then nodded and said, "I've got a feeling that's what happened. I've got a feeling that Inkspot Jones is not just missing, he's dead."

"Is that what you intend to tell Mrs. Jones?"

"Hell, no," Bat said. "That's something I feel, not something I know."

"What *will* you tell her, then?"

"That I'm still looking."

"And where are you going to look?"

"I haven't the faintest idea."

A month went by.

Damon Runyon had to go back to work, and was able to help Bat Masterson only during his free—or stolen—time.

Bat went over old ground, searching Inkspot Jones's desk, his apartment—with the permission of Ida Jones—talking to his friends . . . and coming up empty.

The police had also come up empty, until New Year's Eve, when a body floated to the surface of the Hudson River—or what was left of a body.

Apparently, it had been dumped into the river with weights secured to its ankles, and the water had been cold enough to preserve it to some degree. Still, there had been some decomposition, and while the ankles stayed at the bottom, what was left had risen to the top.

Bat Masterson was at Bellevue Hospital while the autopsy was going on. He had been summoned there by Lieutenant Charles Becker, who did so out of a compassion Bat might not have thought him capable of.

"Mrs. Jones has supplied us with certain medical records that will help us determine if this carcass is Inkspot Jones. I think it would be better for Mrs. Jones if you broke the news to her without her having to come down here," Becker had explained to him.

"*If* this body turns out to be her husband."

Becker only gave Bat a pitying look at that point and then went into the room where the autopsy was being performed, leaving Bat to wait out in the hallway. While he was waiting, Damon Runyon showed up.

"What are you doing here?"

Runyon grinned and said, "Researching an article on new autopsy techniques."

"Sure."

They waited together until Lieutenant Becker came out. He frowned at Runyon, then ignored him and looked at Bat.

"Well?"

"Near as we can tell," he said, "it's Jones."

Section Three

Bat Masterson, Gun-Toter

Pretty much everything we do is more or less of a gamble.

—Bat Masterson, June 18, 1911
The New York Morning Telegraph

CHAPTER NINE

New York
February 1912

Inkspot Jones's death changed things.

Especially since it turned out to be murder.

Inkspot had been shot several times—as near as could be figured—and then dumped in the river with weights tied to his ankles. In most countries, that's called murder.

The detective team of Masterson & Runyon dissolved itself at Inkspot's funeral, and stayed dissolved until the first day of February.

At the funeral they had agreed that looking for a missing person was one thing, but investigating a homicide was something else again.

And Lieutenant Charles Becker had made that abundantly clear to them.

During January and February there were also some changes made in city government. Mayor Gaynor had bowed to public uproar over corruption in the police department. The axe fell on Commissioner Cropsey, whom Gaynor forced to resign. In his place he appointed the forty-five-year-old ex–fire commissioner, a man who knew absolutely nothing about police work, Rhinelander Waldo. Waldo—who some people referred to as a "socialite"—was generally regarded as a man with high ideals, and although he personally was above being corrupted, he was totally beneath Gaynor's thumb.

He also had the wrong impression of the men working under him, unrealistically considering all of them to be men of integrity, while the public knew that the police department was almost entirely corrupt. Because he was in the dark, Waldo had a special way of dealing with corruption complaints. He would assign the accused men to investigate themselves. They were quick to prove themselves innocent of any wrongdoing.

Another move Waldo made was to assign Lieutenant Charles Becker to head up a "strong-arm" squad and to increase his pressure on gambling and prostitution. Becker was to be accountable only to Waldo.

This cut into the time that Becker had to devote to investigating Inkspot Jones's death, and the assignment fell to other men who, although they might have been less corrupt than Becker, were certainly less competent.

On the first day of February, Bat Masterson had breakfast with his wife, who started talking about poor Ida Jones in that tone of voice again.

"Emma, I know where this is leading," Bat said, holding his hands up.

"Bat—"

"The answer is no." He was firm. "I was a total failure looking for a missing person. How do you think I'd do investigating a murder? The police are trained for that—some of them, anyway."

"I told Ida I'd ask—"

"Tell her you asked." Bat stood up to leave. As much as he would have liked to see Inkspot's killer hunted down, he didn't think he was qualified to do it. He started for the door, then stopped abruptly as a thought struck him.

"What's wrong?"

"I'm thinking that maybe I should try to avoid Damon Runyon today."

"Why?"

"Because the last time you and I had a conversation like this, *he* and I had one just like it, and I ended up as a Pinkerton detective."

"You still are."

Soon after Inkspot's body had been found, Bat's detective license had arrived. He had tucked it away in his wallet, where it stayed.

"Only on paper."

"Well," Emma said, giving him a sad look, "I told poor Ida I'd ask. . . ."

Bat glared at his wife for a moment, and then his expression softened. He kissed her forehead and said, "We'll see."

Bat went about his business that day, checking out a new heavyweight kid at the Forty-second Street Gym, working on his column that would come out the next day, Tuesday, and sitting in on the meetings the vice-president of a newspaper must sit in on. All the while he knew that when he saw Runyon, the younger man would try to talk him into investigating Inkspot Jones's murder.

He also spent most of the day wondering why he shouldn't. After all, he *was* technically a Pinkerton detective, and the police had been working on it for a month without any success. He wondered if Becker—or anyone else—had even bothered to talk to Rosenthal, Kelly, or Zelig about it at all. True, Inkspot was a sports reporter, but that didn't mean that he couldn't have run across something on the crime side that he decided to work on—or turn into money.

During the time that had passed since Inkspot's body was discovered, Bat had gone over in his mind that conversation he'd had at Billy's, with Damon Runyon. Presupposing that Inkspot had found out something that he could turn into money, why did it have to be about Rosenthal? It could have been about Kelly, or Zelig—Christ, even about Big Tim Sullivan himself!

Bat knew that Becker had a relationship with Rosenthal—a business relationship—but would he bother to try to hang a murder on him, or either of the other men? The others, perhaps, but putting Rosenthal away would cut into Becker's own profits, and he had never been a particular friend of Inkspot's.

And if Sullivan *was* involved in even the smallest way, would he pressure Commissioner Waldo to kill the whole investigation? He certainly had the power to do it if he so desired, and Waldo, an ex-Army man not known for his backbone, would probably do just that.

So, putting it all together, there was a good possibility that *nobody* was really looking into Inkspot Jones's murder—and *somebody* should!

Before leaving for the day, Bat stopped by the desk of Malcolm Wood, one of the crime reporters on the *Morning Telegraph*.

"How are you, Bat?"

Wood was in his forties and dressed reasonably well for a crime reporter. Bat always felt that those fellas working the street tried to dress so they'd blend in.

"Fine, Malcolm. I was just wondering how the police were coming on Inkspot's murder."

"Why don't you ask your friend Becker?"

Bat and Wood had never socialized, and the crime reporter was no doubt wondering what was going on.

"I'm trying to stay away from him for a while. What do you know about it?"

"I know everything the police know," Wood said, straightening his desk out preparatory to leaving for the evening.

"Which is?"

"Nothing."

"Nothing?"

"They haven't got a clue."

"Have they talked to the big three?" He was referring of course to Rosenthal, Kelly, and Zelig.

"Not that I've heard."

"What about Sullivan?"

"Why him?"

"Why not?"

"That'd be playing with fire, Bat," Wood said, gathering up whatever materials he was taking home with him. Before heading for the door, he added, "Would *you?*"

Bat scowled and said, under his breath, "I may have to."

He went to the Metropole early and did something he hardly ever did—he had dinner there. He wanted to catch Damon Runyon as soon as he entered, and before any of their other drinking buddies arrived.

"You feeling all right tonight?" George Considine asked when Bat asked for a table and said he'd be having dinner.

"Fine."

"Shanley's burn down?"

Early on, it had bothered Considine that Bat would eat at Shanley's and come to the Metropole afterward, but he had long since accepted many of his friends' idiosyncrasies, including that one.

"No, Shanley's did not burn down. Is there something wrong with your kitchen?"

"I have the finest kitchen in New York."

"Then bring me a rare steak and stop questioning me. Can't a fella eat dinner where he wants?"

"One rare steak coming up," Considine said, shaking his head.

Bat was finishing his dinner—the steak had actually not been too bad—when Damon Runyon entered and, spotting Bat Masterson, stopped short. Bat waved him over.

"You're eating here?" Runyon asked.

"Sit down."

"Actually, I'm glad you're here," Runyon said, removing his coat and placing it over Bat's on one of the empty chairs. Seating himself he said, "I want to talk to you about something—"

"Save your breath."

"What?"

"Our detective partnership is back on, if you can work it out."

"How did you know—" Runyon started to ask, frowning.

"Never mind that. Can you get free?"

"Actually, since it's a murder we're talking about, I can probably get myself assigned to it. My paper would love to break this case."

Bat frowned suddenly as he realized something and said, "Hey, so would mine."

Runyon looked at him and said, "We're going to have to work that out, I guess."

"Maybe," Bat said, "but let's worry about it after we find the killer."

"Do you really think we can?"

"Somebody has to. Do you know anyone better qualified?" Before Runyon could reply, Bat said, "Never mind, don't answer that. Order something to eat. The food here's actually not too bad."

The first thing they did was clean out Inkspot Jones's desk at the *Morning Telegraph*, taking all the notes they could find, and then did the same at his residence in the Essex Hotel. Bat was convinced that whatever Inkspot had found out that had gotten him killed must have come as a result of something he was working on. They boxed it all and took it to Bat's own apartment, where Emma immediately offered to go through it for him.

"I want to help," she said simply.

Bat's initial reaction was to tell her no, but then he thought twice and said, "Why not? Maybe you'll see something that I'm missing."

The next thing Bat did he had hoped to be able to do without Emma's seeing him, but since she was there it couldn't be helped. He walked to a dresser, opened a drawer, took out something wrapped in cloth, and put it on the dresser top.

"Bat—" Emma said, but she didn't go any further as Bat unwrapped the item, which turned out to be a gun, a .45. Runyon recognized it as a Peacemaker model, and one that had been kept in good working order.

Also in the drawer was another gun, but Bat left it where it was. That was his Colt Frontier Model 1873 revolver. It was silver-plated, pearl-handled, carved with a Mexican eagle, and marked "W. B. Masterson."

Bat turned and looked at his wife, but she simply gave him an encouraging —but worried—look and remained silent. He considered dropping the gun into his overcoat pocket, but tucked it into his belt instead and buttoned his jacket over it.

"There he is again," he said, mocking himself, "the old gun-toter himself."

"That's a little obvious," Runyon said.

"I hope so."

He and Runyon left Emma eagerly going through Inkspot's papers.

"What's next?" Runyon asked.

Bat looked at Runyon and said, "You're not going to like it."

Runyon stopped just as they were leaving Bat's building and put his hand on Bat's arm. "Do I have to go see Rosenthal again?"

"Maybe," Bat said, "but if you do, I'll be going with you."

Runyon thought that over and said, "I can handle that. What's the bad part?"

"We'll probably have to go and see Zelig and Kelly as well."

"Together?"

Bat nodded, but Runyon knew there was something else.

"And?"

"And Tim Sullivan."

"*Big* Tim Sullivan?"

"I don't think the police have been anywhere near him, Al, and I think one of those men has to be involved. Nobody else would have the nerve to kill a reporter, not in this day and age."

"All right," Runyon agreed, "but is that all?"

"I'm afraid not."

"Who else are we going to talk to?" Runyon asked. "The president of the United States?"

"Close," Bat said. "Very close."

Actually, there was a United States president involved, but it was a *former* president, and they weren't going to talk to him, they were sending him a telegram.

"I'd heard stories about you going to the White House when Roosevelt was president," Runyon said as Bat composed his telegram at the nearest Western Union station.

"Teddy and I have been friends awhile," Bat said, "though we haven't seen each other much since he left office."

"Why write to him now, though?"

"I need him to pave the way for us to talk to someone."

"Sullivan?"

"No," Bat said, handing the message to the clerk and paying him after the man had counted the words. "Not Tim Sullivan."

"Somebody else?" Runyon asked. "Don't we have enough problems?"

"You never have enough problems, lad," Bat said, putting his hand on Runyon's shoulder. "There's always more just around the corner."

"All right, who this time?"

"The police commissioner."

"Waldo?"

Bat nodded. "Rhinelander Waldo."

CHAPTER TEN

From the list of luminaries that Bat had outlined for Runyon, the first man he wanted to talk to was Lieutenant Charles Becker.

"And I'd better see him alone."

"I'll wait for you at Palmer's," Runyon said, referring to a small bar on Grand Street.

Bat went to police headquarters, on Centre Street between Broome and Grand streets. The headquarters building was squeezed onto a too small lot, eighty-eight feet wide at its widest, and forty-six feet at its slimmest point. Although generally considered a fine piece of architecture, it was too crowded in on all sides by the buildings that surrounded it for one even to step back and take a good look.

As head of the Rhinelander Waldo's strong-arm squad, Becker had his own office on the second floor. Bat, knowing right where it was, walked there unchallenged and knocked on the door. Several people turned to look at him, recognizing him, but none challenged his right to be there.

The door was open, and when Bat knocked on it, Becker looked up, saw him, and frowned.

"Is this the commissioner's office?" Bat asked as he entered.

"You got the wrong place," Becker said. "Try two floors up."

"Nice office, Charles," Bat said, looking around the small room.

"It's a hole, but since you're complimenting it, I gather you want something."

"You know me so well, Charles, I don't know why I try."

"Sure," Becker said. "If you want to know what we've got on your friend's murder, the answer is nothing."

"That's partially why I'm here."

"Really? What's the other part?"

Bat spotted the coffeepot in the corner. "Is that full?"

"Might be a cup or two left," Becker said, sitting back. "Help yourself." He decided to let Bat get to the point at his own pace. He needed the break.

Bat squeezed a cup out of the pot, a cup he actually had no intention of drinking. He took it to the chair in front of Becker's desk and sat down.

"All right, Bat, let's get to it."

"I want to talk to Waldo and I'd like you to arrange it."

"Talk to Waldo?" Becker asked, frowning. "Why? About what?"

"About . . . Inkspot Jones's murder."

Becker sat forward and said, "What are you trying to pull? You agreed to stay away from this."

"You're right," Bat said. "I did—a month ago, but the police haven't come up with anything, Charles."

"And you think you can?"

"I think that if *I* start looking, at least I'll know that *somebody* is."

"Bat—"

"Don't get yourself all upset," Bat said, sitting forward and putting the cup of coffee on the desk. "I'm not questioning your abilities."

"What are you doing, then?"

"I know the kind of caseload you must have. In fact, as head of the strong-arm squad, you're not even working on the murder, are you?"

"I'm keeping an eye on the investigation for Commissioner Waldo, just as I was doing when we thought Jones was only missing. The commissioner is concerned when a member of the press comes to harm."

"Well, that's encouraging, but you see what I mean, Charles. You're the only policeman I really have any regard for, and the bulk of your energies is being directed elsewhere."

"Bat, you're going to get yourself in trouble."

"Can you set it up?"

Becker remained silent, drumming his fingers on his desk.

"I can do it without you, Charles."

"How?" Becker asked.

Bat reached into his jacket pocket and brought out a yellow Western Union sheet.

"I've seen your Pinkerton telegram, Bat. You must have your license by now, but that won't get you in to see Waldo."

"This is a new one, Charles," Bat said, handing the policeman the telegram.

Becker resignedly reached across the desk, accepted, read it, and, in spite of himself, was impressed. "President Roosevelt?"

"I'm sure you know that he was once president of the old New York Board of Police Commissioners," Bat said. That was before New York began having only one police commissioner.

"I know that."

"And I'm sure he and Waldo are acquainted."

"They don't like each other," Becker said, handing the telegram back.

"That's why I'd like for you to arrange for me to see Waldo."

Becker nodded as Bat put the telegram away. "If Roosevelt did it, Waldo would talk to you, but he wouldn't be happy about it."

"Happy? He'd be downright hostile."

Becker pointed at Bat and said, "So that little piece of paper was strictly for my benefit?"

"Not necessarily. I understand Sullivan was a Roosevelt man."

"Sullivan?" Becker snapped. "Bat, if you go to Sullivan you're on your own."

Bat said soothingly, "I only asked you to help me with Waldo."

Becker sat back and rubbed his jaw. "All right, I'll talk to him and see what he says. I'll get in touch with you, but give me some time."

"Good enough," Bat said, standing up.

"Hey, aren't you gonna drink the coffee?" Becker asked as Bat made for the door.

"Are you nuts? That stuff looks like mud."

"You're a good judge of coffee."

After Bat left, Becker eyed the phone on his desk. There weren't a whole lot of phones in New York, but he had one, and the commissioner had one. He could have called him right then and there and tried to set up the meeting, but he decided to think about his approach first. Then, when he decided how to do it, he'd do it in person.

He reached for the cup of coffee Bat had left and drank it himself.

Damon Runyon saw Bat enter Palmer's and ordered him a beer.

"Hey," the bartender said, putting the beer on the bar, "ain't you Bat Masterson?"

"No," Bat said, "I'm Wyatt Earp. My friend and I would like to talk, if you don't mind."

"Sure, Mr. Earp, sure," the bartender said, staring at Bat in awe. He moved to the end of the bar and continued to stare.

"What happened?"

"Becker agreed to set up a meeting between me and Waldo," Bat said, grabbing the beer.

"Willingly?"

"I showed him the telegram."

"He would have done it without that, wouldn't he?"

Bat drank some beer and shrugged. "I don't know, but this way he didn't have to make that decision. He's Waldo's fair-haired boy, and he'd prefer to keep his boss happy. Hearing from President Roosevelt would *not* make Rhinelander Waldo happy."

"How's Waldo going to feel about talking to you—or is it us?"

"Sorry, but it's me."

"That's fine with me."

"Waldo won't be happy with what I've got to say, but that's something that he and I are just going to have to deal with when the time comes."

"What *are* you going to say?"

"I haven't quite figured that out yet," Bat said, "but I'm sure the old cuss ain't going to like it."

"When is this momentous meeting supposed to take place?"

"He'll let me know."

Runyon finished his own beer and put the empty mug down on the bar. Bat still had half of his left.

"Well, who do we talk to next? Rosenthal? Kelly?"

"Nobody."

"Nobody?"

Bat shook his head. "Before I talk to any of those people, I want to talk to Waldo. I want him to know what I'm doing, just in case."

"Just in case of what?"

Bat finished his beer and set his mug down. "Just in case the sky falls down and hits me on the head."

By that time the bartender had snuck back over near them, and now he asked, "Would you like another beer, Mr. Earp?"

"No thanks."

"It's on the house."

Bat looked at the man, then at Runyon, and said, "For my friend, too?"

"Sure, of course."

"All right then, one more."

As the bartender went off to fetch them, Bat said under his breath—to his old comrade, Wyatt Earp—"Well, old friend, I always said you were good for nothing. It looks like I was wrong."

Bat and Runyon separated outside of Palmer's, Runyon going home to Flushing and Bat going to the Metropole to see who was there. He found Tom O'Rourke, Val O'Farrell, and William Lewis.

"Well, the long-lost newspaperman," Lewis said, standing up.

"Hello, Will," Bat said, sitting down. "Going home already?"

"Some of us have to work, Bat," Lewis said. "I've got to get back to the office. There's a war brewing in the Balkans any minute, and I want to make sure we get it into print first."

"Why don't we just hope there isn't one?" Bat asked.

"Well, of course we hope that," Lewis said, thrown off balance for a moment, "and if that's the way it goes, we'll be first with that, too."

"You've got ink in your veins, Will."

"Every newsman does," Lewis said. "Don't kid yourself, Bat. See you gentlemen tomorrow," he said to O'Rourke and O'Farrell, and then turned to Bat and added, "You, too, Mr. Masterson."

"Enjoy your war, Will."

As Lewis started walking away, O'Rourke rose and said, "I've got to get along, too. What have you been up to, Bat? Have you heard about this new Zane Grey novel, *Riders of the Purple Sage?*"

"I don't read novels about the West, Tom. You know that."

"This one is supposed to be very accurate in its depictions."

"I'll take your word for it."

"I haven't read it, but when I do I'll tell you all about it."

"Fine."

"Here, while you have time, read this," O'Rourke said, dropping a copy of *Life* magazine in Bat's lap as he passed him. "It's got all of the new slang words in it that people are using today. Learn them and drop them into your speech every once in a while. It'll make you modern."

Bat looked down at the page the magazine was folded to and spotted words and phrases like *peachy!*, *flossy!*, *beat it!*, and *getting your goat.*

"Getting whose goat?" he asked.

"Read it and find out," O'Rourke said. "It's just *peachy.*"

As O'Rourke took his leave, Bat tossed the magazine onto the table and asked Val O'Farrell, "I suppose you have to leave, too?"

"No, I've got nowhere to go," the dapper detective said. "You want a drink?"

"I thought nobody would ever ask."

O'Farrell signaled for a waiter and ordered Bat a beer.

"Where's George?" Bat asked, looking around for George Considine.

"He said something about paperwork."

The waiter brought Bat's beer and Bat took it, saying to O'Farrell, "I'm glad you're here. I've got something I want to talk to you about."

"Oh? What's that?"

"Detective work."

O'Farrell smiled and said, "I heard you were looking for Inkspot Jones a while back, while he was assumed missing."

"Not too successfully, I'm afraid, but I hope to do better this time."

"This time?"

"I'm looking into his murder."

"Well, that's very interesting."

Bat looked at O'Farrell and asked, "You're not working on that, are you?"

"No, I've got enough of a caseload without adding a murder that will never be solved."

"Why do you say that?"

"He was missing for so long, Bat. There's no physical evidence on the body, except to determine that he was shot, and any trail he might have left is long cold. If you're launching your career as a detective on this one, don't get too frustrated."

"I'm not launching a career, Val," Bat said, "I just think someone should be looking. A man's been killed, and *someone* should care."

"He was your friend."

"Yes, and his wife is my wife's friend. That has a lot to do with it, I admit."

"Well, what do you want to do, pick my brains?"

"If I can."

"Consider them yours."

For the next hour Bat alternately talked and asked questions, telling O'Farrell what he intended to do in certain situations, *asking* him what to do in others, and through it all O'Farrell listened and answered very patiently, buying drinks the whole time.

When Bat had finally wound down, O'Farrell asked, "Would you like me to work with you on this?"

"No," Bat said immediately. He'd been expecting the question. "This could be a career breaker, Val, and I don't want to contribute to that. I'm going to rustle a bunch of feathers."

"Feathers that I'd like to see rustled," O'Farrell added, "even Waldo's. I wish I could see that. Remember me if you decide you need some help, will you?"

"You've done enough, Val," Bat said, standing up. "Thanks for the advice, and the drinks."

"Bat," O'Farrell said, stopping him before he could walk away.

"Yes?"

"Be very careful. The people you're going to be dealing with won't be impressed with your reputation. You're going to have to make damn sure that they're impressed with the Bat Masterson they see."

"I'll do my best."

"Do you intend to use that cannon?" O'Farrell asked, indicating the bulge at the front of Bat's jacket.

"It's a—what do you call it? To change people's minds?"

"Deterrent?"

"That's it, a deterrent."

"Do you still remember how to use it?"

Bat looked horrified. "Jesus, I hope so."

CHAPTER ELEVEN

For three days there was no word from Becker about the meeting. War broke out in the Balkans, Tom O'Rourke's opinion of *Riders of the Purple Sage* was high, and Val O'Farrell made a heavy arrest, adding to his laurels. Bat and Runyon met each night at the Metropole, sharing a table with their cohorts, but they were always the last to leave.

When Bat returned from lunch on that third day he was back at his desk only a few moments when William Lewis came out and tapped him on the shoulder.

"You have a phone call in my office."

"A phone call?" Bat made a face. Telephones bothered him, disembodied voices traveling through a long, thin wire. He was much more comfortable with telegrams.

"Come on, come on, take the call and stop tying up my phone."

"Oh, sorry," Bat said. "You must be expecting a call from the queen of England or something."

"I use the thing for business, damn it, not small talk," Lewis muttered as he followed Bat to his office.

Bat entered the office, regarded the instrument doubtfully for a moment, and then lifted the receiver and put it to his ear. He picked up the main body of the phone and spoke into its mouth. "Masterson."

"Bat, it's Becker," a tinny voice said. It didn't even sound like him. "You got your meeting."

"When?"

"Tomorrow, three o'clock."

"His office?"

"Right, fourth floor. Satisfied?"

"You get yourself in trouble?"

"No, and don't you get me in trouble either, Bat."

"I won't."

"And do me a favor."

"What?"

"Lose that cannon."

There was a click in his ear, and Bat handed both sections of the phone to Lewis, saying, "Here, take it."

"Hang it up, for chrissake," Lewis said, taking it and placing it on his desk, putting the pieces together.

Bat rubbed his hands together, as if trying to brush away the feel of a dead animal or something.

"What was that about?"

"Business, Will, just business."

Bat left his office early that day because he wanted to get to Eighth Avenue before Hymie's Gun Shop closed.

"Hey, Bat Masterson," Hymie exclaimed as Bat entered his store. "Don't tell me you're getting back into guns, Bat?"

"Not a chance."

Hymie was a portly man with long muttonchops that were supposed to make up for his bald pate. He was wearing a white shirt with the sleeves rolled up, and a brown vest. The shirt was soiled in spots by gun oil.

"What brings you to my shop?"

"I need a shoulder harness."

"With what kind of gun?"

"No gun," Bat said, unbuttoning his coat and taking the Peacemaker from his belt. "It's got to hold this one."

Hymie stared at the piece, which was nearly forty years old, and he knew that it had seen a lot being carried around for all that time by Bat Masterson.

"You wouldn't want to sell this, would you?" His tone was hopeful.

"No," Bat said. He'd sold some of the guns he'd owned over the years—some of them to Hymie when he first came to New York—but he wanted to keep the Peacemaker. "Just get me a rug for it."

"I don't think I have one that will fit," Hymie said, but then he brightened and said, "Wait."

He vacated the counter and went into his back room while Bat waited patiently. He had no intentions of "losing the cannon" as Becker had asked, but he wasn't going to wear it quite so obviously when he had his meeting with Commissioner Rhinelander Waldo.

When Bat met Damon Runyon at the Metropole that night, he was carrying his "cannon" underneath his left arm in a holster that had been cut away to accommodate it. Hymie had suggested cutting down the barrel of the .45 to make *it* fit the holster, but when Bat had looked properly shocked at the suggestion, the gun dealer quickly suggested cutting away a small portion from the bottom of the holster.

It had worked fine, only it felt like a huge growth that he should have been taking medication to get rid of.

They drank and talked with O'Rourke, Muldoon, and Rickard, and when those three left, Runyon leaned forward and asked, "What happened to the gun?"

"It's there."

Runyon frowned, examined Bat, and then said, "Where?"

Bat opened his coat and pulled back his jacket on the left to show the younger man the gun.

"Holy . . ." Runyon said. "How does it feel?"

"Like a growth."

"Haven't you ever worn a gun there before?"

Bat laughed mirthlessly and said, "Sure, but not a Peacemaker."

"Why now?"

"I don't want to scare the commissioner."

"You got the meeting?"

Bat nodded. "Got a call from Becker this afternoon. It's set up for tomorrow at three in Waldo's office."

Runyon pursed his lips and then said, "Do you know what you're going to say?"

"Not really."

"You're not going to accuse him of bowing to political pressure, are you?"

"If I did, it wouldn't be the first time somebody had accused him," Bat said. "But no, that wouldn't be the way to get on his better side."

"From what I hear," Runyon said, "he doesn't have one."

"If I find one, I'll let you know."

Rhinelander Waldo was the butt of many jokes in the Police Department. The sad thing was that he didn't really know it. Bat felt that he wasn't only incompetent, but very possibly stupid as well. Still, Gaynor had control of him, but what Bat wanted to know was, did Big Tim Sullivan own him, too?

Bat arrived at headquarters fifteen minutes early and entertained the thought of stopping in on Becker, but decided against it. Maybe afterward . . .

It was funny, Bat thought, Waldo picking Becker to be his right-hand man. Bat and Becker were friends, but Bat knew that Becker had his hands in a lot of pockets, and obviously Waldo had no idea at all.

Walking up to the fourth floor it struck Bat that in outlining to Damon Runyon the people they'd have to see, he'd left one out, and now he wondered why. Of course, that was Mayor Gaynor himself, and depending on how the meeting with Waldo went, the mayor just might have to be added to the list.

On the fourth floor he presented himself to the commissioner's clerk, a youthful-looking patrolman who was obviously impressed. Nervously, he told Bat to wait a moment and he'd announce his presence to the commissioner.

When the man came back he said, "Come this way, please, sir."

"Sure, son."

Bat followed the patrolman to a pair of oak doors, which the young man opened and then stepped aside.

"Bat Masterson, sir," the man announced.

As Bat entered, Waldo stood up from behind his desk and waited. He was a slender, dark-haired man, who looked as if he'd be more at home at a tea party than in the police commissioner's office.

"Mr. Masterson," the man said as Bat approached the desk. He stuck his hand out, and Bat took it and shook it.

"Commissioner."

"We've never met, of course, but I've heard a lot about you. I read your columns as well."

"Thank you, Commissioner."

Waldo frowned and said, "I understand you're friends with President Roosevelt?"

"I have that honor, yes."

"Ah, well . . ." Waldo said, as if indicating that he would have to forgive Bat his bad taste in friends. Bat held his temper in check.

"I understand from Lieutenant Becker that you have something you'd like to talk to me about?"

"That's right."

"Well, have a seat and we'll get to it," Waldo said, seating himself.

Bat sat down and studied Waldo for a few moments, trying to choose his words carefully. Finally he decided simply to speak his mind.

"Commissioner, I'm investigating the murder of Delaney Jones."

"Jones?"

"The newsman who was fished out of the Hudson sometime back—"

"Wasn't he the fellow who was missing for a while?" Waldo asked with a frown, interrupting him.

"That's him."

"And you're investigating, you say?" the commissioner was plainly puzzled. "I was under the impression that you were a newspaperman, Mr. Masterson."

"Yes, sir, I am," Bat said, "but I'm also a Pinkerton operative."

"Are you licensed?"

"I am," Bat said, reaching for his pocket.

Waldo held up his hand to stop him and said, "If you say so, I'll take your word for it."

Trusting, Bat thought. An admirable trait, but not in a police commissioner.

"Why have you come to me with this piece of information?" Waldo asked. "I hope you're not asking me to approve?"

"No, I'm not, Commissioner," Bat said, shifting in his chair. "I guess what I'm really asking you to do is not get in my way."

"How do you mean that?" Apparently, Waldo was unsure as to whether or not he should take offense.

"I'm going to have to talk to a few people who might not like it, Commissioner, and you might get some pressure."

"What people? What kind of pressure?"

"Political pressure, I guess I mean."

"I don't bow to pressure, Mr. Masterson," Waldo said stiffly. "Who are these people you'll be talking to?"

Bat gave him the names, watching his face carefully. Either the man truly didn't react when he heard Tim Sullivan's name, or he was a damned good actor. He did react, however, when Bat spoke the name of Mayor Gaynor.

"I wouldn't want you bothering the mayor, Mr. Masterson."

"I'm hoping I won't have to, Commissioner."

"Tell me something, Masterson. Why are you getting involved in this?"

"Delaney Jones was my friend."

"Is that all?"

"No, sir. I don't believe his death is being looked into properly."

Waldo rose to the defense of his department. "Are you accusing my men of behaving improperly?"

"I'm saying that maybe they're not as concerned as I am about finding his killer."

"Mr. Masterson," Waldo said, rising to his feet, "I don't appreciate having the integrity of my men impugned."

Bat frowned, not sure what the man meant by that, but he thought he could guess. Waldo was still one of the only people in New York who linked the word "integrity" with his corruption-torn department.

Bat rose and said, "I think I've said my piece, Commissioner."

"I believe you have," Waldo said coldly. "Good day to you, sir."

Bat turned and walked to the double doors, but when he reached them, instead of going out he turned to face the commissioner again. "One more thing, Commissioner."

"What's that?"

"I don't bow to pressure either," Bat said, opening the doors. "I just thought you ought to know."

They met in Palmer's again, this time taking a back table. The bartender came with their beers and popped his eyes at Bat again.

"Twice in one week, Mr. Earp," the man said. "I'm honored. I've read all about you—"

"That's fine," Bat said, cutting the man off. "I'll give you an autograph on the way out."

"Great!"

"Only let's keep it our little secret, eh?"

"Sure, Mr. Earp, sure."

The man backed away, and Runyon looked at Bat. "How did it go?"

"I don't know," Bat said honestly. "I told him what I had to tell him and he told me what he had to tell me."

"Did you get the impression that he was getting pressure?"

"Yeah, but not from where we thought," Bat said. "He didn't flinch when I said Sullivan's name, but he did when I said the mayor's."

"The mayor?"

"We all know he's under the mayor's thumb," Bat said. "If the mayor told him to kill an investigation, Waldo would kill it just like that."

"But why would the mayor—"

"Maybe it's Mayor Gaynor who gets the pressure from higher up. Why couldn't Big Tim Sullivan pull the mayor of New York's strings?"

"Gaynor's got political ambitions, doesn't he?" Runyon said, getting into the spirit of things.

"And helping Tim Sullivan sure wouldn't hurt, would it?"

"Not one bit," Runyon said. "You going to talk to Gaynor next?"

"I guess I should," Bat said, "but he might be harder to get to than Waldo was."

"Can't you use President Roosevelt?"

"I could, and I might when the time comes, but I might have to wait a few more days before I can get in to see Gaynor, and I want to get started on the others. Besides, we might not have to ask Gaynor if he's getting pressure from Sullivan."

"Why not?"

Bat looked at him and said, "We might be able to get the answer to that from Sullivan himself."

"Is that who we're seeing first?"

"Why not? He prides himself on being available to his constituents." Bat stood up and said, "Let's go and knock on the door of Tammany Hall."

CHAPTER TWELVE

The first Tammany Society was formed on May 1, 1772, in Philadelphia. It was named after the Indian chief Tammanend, who aided in the purchase of a portion of Philadelphia when he signed a treaty with William Penn.

During the Revolutionary War the name Tammany came to stand as a symbol of liberty. Other societies cropped up around the country, and naturally one of them was in New York.

Over the years—and due largely to the influence of "Boss" Tweed, possibly the most famous of the Tammany leaders—Tammany Hall had become involved in politics and corruption, two things that seemed to go hand in hand.

The present Tammany Hall leader was one Big Tim Sullivan, and he was carrying on the tradition of Boss Tweed very competently.

The Tammany Hall Society's headquarters was on Fourteenth Street, but Sullivan himself lived in a mansion on Thirty-eighth and Lexington, a house that had once been the home of Tammany leader "Honest John" Kelly, also known as "Boss" Kelly, toward the end of the nineteenth century.

Bat and Runyon dismissed their taximeter cab in front of the house on Thirty-eighth Street and approached the door.

"Somehow, I can't see Inkspot having any connection with someone who would live here," Runyon said as they ascended the front steps.

"If there is a connection, it's got to be indirect."

Bat knocked on the door and waited, then knocked again, both times using a huge brass knocker made in the shape of an angel.

The door was answered on the second knock by a man dressed all in black. "Yes, can I help you?"

"We'd like to speak to Mr. Sullivan, please," Bat said.

"May I ask your names?"

"Bat Masterson and Damon Runyon."

If the man recognized either of their names, he gave no outward sign. "Please wait."

They had waited a few moments, studying the front of the house with interest, when the door was opened again by the same man.

"Come this way, please."

He turned and walked into the house, and they followed. Runyon took up the rear and closed the door behind them.

The servant led them through a large entry hall to a lavishly furnished office, where a man sat behind a huge desk, looking for all the world like a king in his castle.

"Mr. Masterson, Mr. Runyon," the man greeted, standing up. Tim Sullivan was a big, good-looking man with wavy gray hair and penetrating blue eyes. One of the innovations he had brought to Tammany Hall was the practice of calling himself "Big" Tim Sullivan rather than "Boss" Sullivan. It was a practice that would be carried on after him as well.

"Mr. Sullivan," Bat said, moving into the room with Runyon right behind him.

"Oh, call me Big Tim," Sullivan said. "I encourage all my constituents to do so." Sullivan looked past them at the man who had led them there and said, "That will be all, Henry."

"Yes, sir."

Henry backed out of the room and closed the door behind him.

"Have a seat, gentlemen," Sullivan invited. "May I get you a drink?"

"No thanks," Bat said, answering for both of them.

"Well then, what can I do for you?" Sullivan sat, and before Bat could answer he said, "I'm avid readers of both of you, you know."

"Really."

Sullivan took the hint and said, "I see you would like to get down to business."

"That's right."

"Which is?"

"Inkspot Jones."

Sullivan frowned. "Who?"

"Delaney Jones, a newspaperman."

Sullivan still looked puzzled, so Bat said, "Don't tell me you weren't an avid reader of his, too?"

"I'm sorry," Sullivan said, "but I'm confused. Am I supposed to know this man?"

"Maybe not," Bat said. He decided simply to tell Sullivan what he had told Waldo. "He was killed recently, and I'm trying to find out who did it."

"Isn't that a job for the police?"

"They weren't doing too well at it, so I decided to deal myself in."

"I see. Is there some way you think I can help you? Is that why you're here?"

"Maybe," Bat said. "All I really want you to do is tell me anything you know about it."

"That would be very easy," Sullivan said, "since I know nothing about it."

"Fine," Bat said, standing up. It was Runyon's turn to be puzzled now, but he stood up also, waiting to see what Bat would do next.

Bat started for the door, then stopped in mid-stride and said, "Oh, by the way?"

"Yes?"

"I think I'll be calling on some friends of yours, and I'd appreciate their cooperation."

"Who would that be?"

"Herman Rosenthal . . . Jack Zelig . . . Monk Eastman . . . Paul Kelly." Bat paused after each name to observe Sullivan's reactions, but the man had been a politician too long to let his face reveal what he was thinking.

"I know those names, of course," Sullivan said. "They're all rather notorious, but what makes you think I have any contact with them?"

"Rumor."

Sullivan reacted as if Bat had said a dirty word.

"Rumor?" the man said, standing up abruptly. "Why is it everyone believes a rumor when it is about a politician?"

Bat shrugged and said, "I guess they're the most fun to spread rumors about."

"And it's you people," Sullivan said, pointing at them, "you newspaper people who spread them, isn't it? Isn't it?" he shouted, spittle spouting from his mouth and covering his chin.

The door to the room opened and Henry entered. He looked at his boss, and then at Bat and Runyon. "I think you had better leave now."

Bat stared at Sullivan, who was standing there, shaking, his eyes bright and feverish. "I guess we'd better."

He stepped past Henry, who moved aside to let him and Runyon out of the room.

"Please, let yourselves out."

"We'll do that," Runyon said.

He and Bat walked directly to the front door and out. They descended the steps, moved out to the sidewalk in front of the house, and then stopped.

"Jesus," Runyon said.

"That man's crazy," Bat said. "I'd heard stories about him, but now I know it's true. He's going mad."

"What does that mean to us?"

"I guess it means we won't be able to predict what he'll do."

"Think he'll tell the others?" Runyon asked. "Rosenthal and the others?"

"He's supposed to be closest to Kelly," Bat said. "Maybe he'll talk to him. That don't mean that Kelly will tell the others. As for Zelig, he doesn't talk to anybody."

"So, does that mean that Kelly is next?"

Bat looked at Runyon and said, "Yep, Kelly is next . . . tomorrow," Bat said, with finality. "Waldo and Sullivan in one day are enough."

"What about Gaynor?"

"I think I'll get in touch with his office and ask for an appointment through channels," Bat said. "It may take some time, but I won't be idle while I'm waiting, and Gaynor might be a little more willing to talk than if I tried to pressure him into seeing me."

"That makes sense."

They were walking back to Times Square when Runyon suddenly asked, "Why do you say that Sullivan is the closest to Kelly?"

Bat looked at the younger man and said, "Rumor."

Runyon went back to the Gotham while Bat went home to find Emma poring over the papers from Inkspot Jones's desk. She had them spread out on part of the kitchen table.

"Emma, are you still reading those papers?" he said, removing his flat-topped bowler and setting it on the table. It was more of an observation than a question.

"You're so sure the answer is here, Bat," Emma Masterson said.

"I'm not *sure*," Bat said, correcting her. "I just feel it."

"Well, your instincts have been pretty good through the years, so why ignore them now?"

"We've both been over and over that stuff," Bat said. "Is there anything to eat?"

"Why should there be?" she asked. "You didn't tell me you were going to grace me with the pleasure of your company this evening for dinner." Her tone was good-natured, and she didn't look up from her work when she said it.

"No, I suppose I didn't," he said, lowering himself wearily into a chair. God, but he was tired. Did Runyon get this tired? Probably not. He didn't get tired when he was that age.

He got tired a lot lately, though.

Finally looking up at her husband for the first time since he'd arrived, Emma frowned with concern. "Are you all right?"

"Tired," he said. "I'm tired. I saw two powerful men today. One of them is a puppet and the other a madman." Thinking of the mayor, he added, "I'm wondering what I'll find when I talk to the man between them."

Emma stood up and said, "I can make some soup, and some chicken if you like, or I could combine them and make some chicken soup."

"Do I look like an old man who needs chicken soup, woman?" Bat asked, in reality only slightly annoyed. He did *feel* like an old man on this particular night.

"No, but you *sound* like a tired old man," she said, rattling pots as she sorted through looking for the right one. "Some chicken soup and early to bed will do you good, get you back to your old self."

There was that word again, Bat thought.

Old.

"Chicken soup sounds fine."

Lieutenant Charles Becker had problems, not the least of which was his friend Bat Masterson's suddenly deciding to play detective to find a killer—and his intentions were to push the wrong people while doing it.

Not that Becker minded if Bat bothered Herman Rosenthal a little. Since the beginning of the year Becker had seen a change in Rosenthal, and had suspected the gambling boss of cheating him more often than not on his cut of the action. This being the case, Becker was going to have to take steps to show Rosenthal who the real boss was.

Another problem was the case that Becker was building against Jack Zelig. Zelig was a powerful man in New York, with allegiance to no one—not the way Rosenthal owed Becker, and Paul Kelly owed Big Tim Sullivan. However, since Zelig *was* such a powerful man—and would continue to be so even from behind bars—that Becker had lately been thinking he might be able to use Zelig against Rosenthal in the event the problems with Rosenthal escalated.

His decision, then, was to let Zelig walk around a bit longer, even though he might have enough to put the man away, and wait to see how the situation with Rosenthal resolved itself. Besides, there was a possible witness against Zelig whom he was looking for, and when he found him it would strengthen his case even more. There was no harm in waiting, at this point.

Clearing his desk for the trip home, Becker wondered how Bat's meeting with Waldo had gone, and why the old legend hadn't stopped in on him to let him know. Jesus, he hoped Bat would stay away from Big Tim Sullivan. Everybody in the know was aware of the fact that Sullivan was two steps from a nuthouse. If Bat started pushing him about a murdered newspaperman, it might just push Sullivan over the edge. People weren't prepared for that yet. They were close, but they weren't yet totally prepared.

Masterson, Rosenthal, Zelig, problems all, and then there were the daily things, the gambling and prostitution raids that Waldo—the fool—wanted run. So far, Becker had managed to avoid raiding any of Rosenthal's places, but maybe that was in order now.

Yes, Becker thought as he left his office, maybe the time had come for Rosenthal to be squeezed a little.

Idly, as he left headquarters for the trip home, Becker wondered who had actually killed—or ordered killed—Inkspot Jones.

Maybe finding that out would be a useful piece of information to turn to his own advantage.

CHAPTER THIRTEEN

As it was February, baseball was once again making its way into the newspapers. Articles anticipating the coming season, predicting the outcome, began to show up every day. It was for this reason that Damon Runyon was unable to accompany Bat Masterson to his encounter with Paul Kelly.

Bat had some catching up to do himself at his office, and also had to put in his request for an appointment with Mayor Gaynor, but when he finally presented himself in front of Runyon's desk at noon, the younger man gave him the bad news.

"If you could wait until I'm finished with this," Runyon had said to Bat while they sat in his office at the *American*, "I could go with you."

"No," Bat said, standing up. "I want to see Kelly early in the day. People like Kelly are usually night people, and I'm hoping to throw him off balance this way."

"You feel safer seeing him in the daylight?"

"As safe as I can feel."

Runyon wondered idly if Bat was really afraid of anything these days, considering the things he had gone through in his lifetime.

"What will you do after you see Kelly?"

"Move on to the next one."

"Who will that be?"

"Monk Eastman."

"You're saving Rosenthal for last?"

Bat nodded. "I want to hear what the others have to say about him before they get a chance to compare notes."

"By the time you get to him, he may be expecting you," Runyon warned.

Bat smiled patiently and said, "He's already expecting me, Al. I'm keeping him off balance just by making him wait."

Bat started for the door, and Runyon said, "By the way, before you leave—"

"Yeah?"

"Can I quote you on who you think will win the World Series this year?"

"If Marquard repeats his year, the Giants are a sure thing."

"Bat, you of all people know that there's no such thing as a sure thing."

"I of all people," Bat said, deadly serious, "know that there is."

As Bat Masterson left, Damon Runyon had a sneaking suspicion that his last remark had not been about sports.

A mailboy came by Runyon's desk and dropped some letters onto it, but he didn't get around to opening any of them for an hour.

In 1912 the majority of the gambling done in New York City took place from Thirty-third Street to Fifty-ninth, between Third and Eighth avenues. Two years earlier Paul Kelly had opened a place called the New Englander Social and Dramatic Club on Seventh Avenue, just north of what people were calling the Roaring Forties.

Bat knew that Kelly would be there, going over yesterday's take, cutting out the three hundred dollars a month that had to be paid in protection to certain city officials. There were almost half a dozen first-class gambling houses from Fortieth to Fiftieth streets, between Third and Eighth, and they all paid their three hundred dollars a month. That came to a lot of money a month, and Bat knew that his friend Lieutenant Becker was getting his fair share of it—and he couldn't hold that against him. Lord knew, Wyatt Earp got his fair share in Tombstone and other towns across the West, and he never held that against him either. Bat didn't judge his friends, and he hoped that Wyatt was getting his share out in California, too.

He pounded his fist on the door of the New Englander and waited for one of Kelly's well-dressed street mugs to answer. That was the difference between Paul Kelly and Monk Eastman: Kelly dressed his people better. Eastman's minions dressed like what they were, strong-arm mugs.

The door was opened by a man wearing a conservative gray suit that fit him as well as a banana peel would fit a watermelon. "Yeah?" he asked, and his Five Points accent came out full force in that one word.

"I'd like to see Mr. Kelly."

"He's busy."

"No kidding."

"Move along, Pop—" the man started to say, putting his hand out to push Bat away from the door, but as he did so his hand came into contact with the Peacemaker underneath Bat's arm and he shopped short.

"Who are you?" the man asked, narrowing his eyes.

"My name is Bat Masterson, and I'd like to see Paul Kelly . . . please."

He saw the flash of recognition in the man's eyes, and then the speculative look on the man's face as he wondered how much of the old legend was still present.

"Come on, friend," Bat said impatiently—and perhaps a little recklessly—"make a play or back off."

Bat was more in his element dealing with a gunhand like this than with politicians like Waldo and Sullivan. He knew what buttons to push, and he'd pushed the right one.

The man backed off.

"Wait here," he said, retreating and closing the door. Bat allowed him to close the door because he knew he'd be back shortly. Of all the names on his list—Kelly, Eastman, Zelig—Kelly was the one he knew personally, though he could lay no claim to friendship. He was sure that Kelly would see him.

The door opened only moments later, and the same man appeared and said, "Follow me."

The club was dark, but there was a light on in the rear, illuminating several tables. At one of the tables sat Paul Kelly, with stacks of money and paperwork in front of him, and two conservatively dressed mugs standing behind him.

"Redecorating your office, Kelly?"

Kelly looked up at Bat and smiled wolfishly. "Going to put me in your column, Masterson?" he asked, counting out a new stack of bills.

"Not hardly."

"Then, what do you want?"

"To talk."

Kelly studied Bat for a few moments, then said, "Want a drink while you talk?"

"No."

"Can I take your coat?"

"It won't take that long."

"Okay," Kelly said, making a last notation on a sheet of ledger paper and then sitting back. "I could use a break. Go ahead, talk."

"You want to tell this monkey behind me to take a walk?"

"He tells me you're carrying a gun. A big one."

"The streets are unsafe these days."

"Not for a legend like yourself, I'm sure."

"Let's just say I'm getting nervous in my old age."

Kelly looked past Bat and nodded, and the man moved to Bat's left and leaned against the bar. For a moment—just for a fleeting moment—Bat wondered if he would be able to get the gun out and a shot off before any of Kelly's men could react.

There was a time . . .

"What's on your mind?" Kelly asked, breaking into his reverie.

"Inkspot Jones."

"Jones?" Kelly said, frowning. "That name is familiar."

"They fished him out of the Hudson at the beginning of the year."

"A newspaperman, right?"

"That's right."

"I guess he must have written something somebody didn't like. That's an occupational hazard with you fellas, isn't it? I mean, writing things about people the way you do?"

"We don't look at it that way," Bat said. "What about you, Kelly?"

"What do you mean?"

"Did he write something *you* didn't like?"

"Me? I don't even remember what kind of stuff he wrote. What was he, a crime reporter?"

"Sports."

"I don't even like sports, except to bet on now and again." Kelly frowned then as something seemed to occur to him. "Hey, wait a minute. What are you doing here, Masterson? Why are you asking about—"

"I'm looking for Inkspot's killer, Kelly. I figured he found out something he shouldn't and that's what got him killed. What do you think about that?"

"Are you trying to tie me up with that?" Kelly asked incredulously.

"I'm just seeing if you fit, Kelly. You know, like trying on a new suit?"

Kelly seemed to need a few moments to think that over, and while he did, Bat exchanged glances with the men standing behind Kelly—or tried to anyway. Their eyes were rather blank and unfocused. He imagined that they needed some sort of word from their boss to set them off.

"This is interesting," Kelly finally said.

"What is?"

"Who else are you trying this out on? Eastman? Rosenthal? What about Big Jack?"

"You think any of them look good for it?"

"Oh, no," Kelly said, shaking his head, "you're not going to get me to help you pin it on one of them."

"I don't want to pin it on anyone, Paul," Bat said softly. "I want the man who did it."

"Well, one of them will have done it, you know," Kelly said. "I mean, they order their murders done for them."

"Like you do?"

"That's never been proven," Kelly said testily. "I think this conversation has just come to an end."

"Are you going to ask your boys to show me out?" Bat asked, sensing a straightening in the third man standing on his left.

Kelly looked at Bat with interest and said, "Wouldn't that be something to see? How much of the old Bat Masterson is there left, I wonder?"

Bat's heart started to beat more rapidly, but he stood his ground. "Stop wondering and find out."

Kelly considered, then sat forward and said, "No, not today. I'm busy, Masterson. Go and try to hang your murder on somebody else."

"You wouldn't be planning to call ahead, would you? Warn the others?"

"And deprive them of a big laugh? Not a chance."

Bat waited for more, but it wasn't forthcoming as Kelly picked up a stack of money, so he backed away, watching Kelly's men carefully until he reached the front hall, then turned and walked out the door.

Outside he took a moment to catch his breath and noticed that his hands were sweating. What would have happened, he thought, if Kelly *had* stopped wondering after all?

Bat was still wondering a block later when someone touched him on the shoulder.

He whirled around, his hand going to the Peacemaker by reflexes he'd thought—feared—long gone. His coat was open, and it came out smoothly and easily, though not quite as fast as it once had, and he pointed it at Damon Runyon's nose.

"Jesus!" Runyon said, staring down the long barrel of the gun.

"Al!" Bat said, lowering the gun.

Runyon swallowed, moistened his lips, and said, "That was fast."

Bat, feeling embarrassment, hastily holstered the weapon and looked around to see if anyone else had seen. There was an elderly couple walking by, staring at him, and he took hold of Runyon's arm and said, "Come on, let's walk."

"What happened with Kelly to make you so jumpy?"

"Nothing. Old reflexes took over, that's all. What are you doing here? I thought you had work to do."

"This comes under the heading of work," Runyon said as they walked south. "Remember that column I did asking for information about Inkspot?"

"Sure I remember. Nothing ever came of it, did it?"

"No," Runyon said, "until today."

Bat stopped short and asked, "What do you mean?"

"I got a letter a little while ago," Runyon said, taking a small envelope from his pocket. "This letter."

"About Inkspot?"

"Yes."

"Well, what's it say?"

"It's from a woman, Bat."

"A woman?"

"She claims that she and Inkspot were . . . having an affair."

"Inkspot?" Bat asked. "I don't believe it."

"Well, we'll have a chance to ask her to prove it," Runyon said. "She wants to talk to me."

"Why didn't she come forward before?"

"I guess that's one of the things we're going to have to ask her."

"That and a hell of a lot more," Bat said with feeling. "Where does she live?"

"In Brooklyn."

"Brooklyn?" Bat made a face, because going to Brooklyn meant riding an extended distance in an automobile, a practice he tried his best to avoid. But if it had to be done, it had to be done. "Well then," he said, "what are we waiting around here for?"

"I was just waiting until I found you," Runyon said. "And now that I have, let's go."

CHAPTER FOURTEEN

In the taxi to Brooklyn, Runyon told Bat that the woman, who had given her name as Milly Cabot, had not given her home address in her letter.

"Where are we supposed to meet her, then?"

"In the Brooklyn Botanical Gardens."

Bat leaned forward and asked the driver, "Do you know where that is?"

"Yes, sir."

"Well, take us there."

Coming off the Brooklyn Bridge, the driver made his way to Flatbush Avenue, which would take them to Grand Army Plaza. Once they drove around Grand Army Plaza, they would pick up Flatbush Avenue again—as opposed to taking Eastern Parkway, which would have taken them to a part of Brooklyn called East New York. Taking Flatbush Avenue again would take them south to Prospect Park and, across the street from the park, the Brooklyn Botanical Gardens, which had opened in 1910.

The opening of the Botanical Gardens gave Brooklyn a park designed for the display of flowers, fifty acres devoted to rock gardens and water-lily pools, a children's garden and sections of azaleas, dogwoods, forsythia, and what would become Brooklyn's official flower, the rhododendron.

"How are we supposed to recognize her?" Bat asked as they started to follow the circle of Grand Army Plaza around the huge monuments that had been erected in 1866.

Runyon had been staring at the monuments when Bat spoke to him.

"She said she'll be near the children's garden, and that she would find us."

"How is *she* supposed to recognize us—or should I say you?"

Runyon shrugged and said, "That's all that her letter said."

"In this letter," Bat asked, "she didn't happen to mention whether or not her information would be for *sale*, did she?"

Shaking his head, Runyon said, "No. You think she's just out after some money?"

"I might," Bat said, rubbing his chin, "but why did she wait all this time?"

"You're saying that since she did wait all this time that she might be reacting to a guilty conscience?"

"Maybe," Bat said. "Let me see the letter."

Runyon handed it over and said, "That would mean that what she has to tell us is probably true."

Bat took the letter out of the envelope and shook his head. "I can't believe it. Inkspot Jones stepping out on his wife?"

"Well, Ida Jones is a nice woman, Bat, but she's not a raving beauty. It is possible—"

"And what about Inkspot?" Bat asked. "He was my friend, but at his best he still looked like an unmade bed."

"Some women like unmade beds."

"I wonder what *she* looks like," Bat said, giving his attention over to her letter. He read it through, but Runyon had given him all of the contents in a nutshell. It read this way:

Dear Mr. Runyon,

  I had read your column of some time ago and feel that I must now come forward about Delaney Jones's murder. He and I were seeing each other, and if you will meet me at the children's garden at the Botanical Gardens in Brooklyn, I will tell you all I know.

Bat replaced the letter in the envelope and handed it back to Runyon.

"She sounds educated, at least," Runyon said, putting the letter away in his pocket.

"Maybe that will work to our advantage."

The driver dropped them at the entrance to the Botanical Gardens, and they entered together after instructing him to wait. Since it was winter, the park was almost empty.

"Now we know how she'll recognize us," Runyon said. "Who else would be out here in the winter?"

Bat nodded, spotted the sign that directed them to the children's garden, and said, "That way."

They walked along, hands deep inside their coat pockets, taking in the sights, imagining what it would probably look like in the spring, with the flowers all blooming and the place teeming with people.

"Must be a beautiful place when the season's right," Runyon said.

"There," Bat said, inclining his head. Runyon looked and saw a woman standing near the children's garden, apparently studying the ground. As they approached her, she looked up, giving them an opportunity to study her.

She was in her forties, but she was a handsome woman—not a beauty, but certainly more attractive than Ida Jones. Her body, inside a cheap coat and simple dress, was full and womanly. Her face was pleasant, just starting to flesh out from age. Her lips were full, slightly touched with color, but her skin was pale as she wore no other makeup.

As they moved closer to her she began to back away from them, obviously unnerved by the fact that there were two of them instead of one.

"Miss Cabot?" Runyon called out. "I'm Damon Runyon, the man you wrote to." As she continued to back away, he went on. "This is my friend, Bat Masterson. He was a friend of Ink—uh, Delaney Jones's."

At the sound of Bat's name, the woman stopped and stared frankly at him. "He talked about you a lot," she said, speaking directly to Bat.

"We were friends, Miss Cabot. I'm trying to find out who killed him," Bat explained. "Anything you could tell us that might help would be appreciated."

"It's Mrs."

"Beg pardon?"

"It's Mrs. Cabot," the woman said, "not Miss."

"I'm sorry," Bat said. "Mrs. Cabot."

She had stopped retreating, and now she moved toward them. As she got closer, Bat could see that she was probably closer to fifty than forty. Still, she would have been a "younger woman" to Inkspot. Could that have been part of the appeal?

"I'm ashamed," she said.

"Of what?" Bat asked.

"Of what I did."

"You mean," Runyon asked, "having an affair with Delaney Jones? Cheating on your husband?"

Her head jerked up and she looked Runyon in the eye, her own eyes flashing with anger. "I never cheated on my husband, Mr. Runyon," she snapped. "Never!"

"I'm sorry," Runyon said, "but your letter—"

"My husband died five years ago," she explained. "I had been alone for all that time, until I met Delaney."

"Where was that, Mrs. Cabot?"

"At the racetrack."

That Bat could believe. What he couldn't believe was that Inkspot had a woman on the side and had never let on to him about it. Then again, they were friends, but they really didn't see each other *all* the time. They went to the track together once a week, and saw each other at the office, but never actually spent a lot of time talking.

"How long ago?"

"Almost as soon as he came here to New York. We met the first time he went to the track."

They'd been seeing each other for months, then. The fact that the woman did seem to have some education, and that Inkspot was not the smoothest talker around, made the situation all that much more difficult to accept.

"What is it you're ashamed of, then?" Runyon asked.

"That I didn't come forward sooner," she said, lowering her eyes.

"You mean, when his body was discovered?"

"I mean when it was discovered that he was missing," she said, "last year."

"Why *didn't* you come forward?" Bat asked.

She looked at him, and he could see the tears welling in her eyes. "I was afraid," she said with a shrug. "Afraid."

"Of what?"

"He had been talking for some time about making a killing," she said.

"Why would that frighten you?"

"He said that he had something on a very big man in this town, and that he was going to turn it into a lot of money. I was afraid that somebody that big would come after me if I came forward."

Bat found himself leaning toward the woman. "Did he ever say who it was?" he asked, barely containing his eagerness for the answer—for *the* answer, which he did not get.

"No, he never told me the man's name. He said I'd be safer not knowing."

"Did he say what it might be about?"

"He said he had discovered it in the course of his job," she said. "I assumed that meant it had something to do with sports."

Well, that *was* something. At least they knew now that Inkspot hadn't crossed over to the crime beat, but it still didn't rule out Rosenthal, Kelly, and the others. Gamblers that they were, they often took bets on sports. Perhaps, though, this would eliminate the politicians. That remained to be seen.

"Milly, this is very important," Bat said. "When did this business start?"

"A few months before he disappeared."

"Had he been getting any money from the man all along?"

"Small amounts to start with, but he decided that it was time he hit it big."

"Yeah," Bat said, "Inkspot always said he figured he'd hit big one of these days."

"I guess he decided to go about it the wrong way," Runyon said.

"He talked about it for weeks before he disappeared."

"Did you see him the night before he disappeared?"

"No, but I saw him a couple of days before that. He said he wanted to stay away from me until he collected, to keep me safe."

Apparently, Inkspot had known he was playing with fire, and he went ahead with it anyway. What could he have had that was that big?

"Mrs. Cabot, why did you decide to come forward now?" Runyon asked.

A tear rolled out of each eye as she said, "I couldn't bear the guilt anymore. If I had come forward sooner, he might still be alive."

Bat stared at her. Her reasoning was sound—if she had come forward in January, right after his body had been found. But she had still waited two months. Why?

"Milly, there's nothing else you can tell us that might help?" Runyon asked.

She frowned and tried to think of something, but finally gave up and said, "I'm sorry, there's nothing," and started to cry.

Runyon moved close to her and put his hands on her shaking shoulders, trying to calm her.

"See if you can get an address, Al," Bat said, "so we can keep in touch, and make sure she knows where to contact either of us if she thinks of something else."

"All right."

Bat walked away from them, leaving it to Runyon to comfort the weeping woman. He studied the hard ground that in a couple of months would begin to yield beautiful, fragrant flowers. It was beneath hard ground like this that Delaney Jones's remains were buried—all except his feet and ankles, which were probably still at the bottom of the Hudson, chained to whatever had been used to weight him down in the first place.

Well, it was a fact now, if this woman was to be believed. Inkspot had stumbled onto something, and it had to do with someone big. The list of names Bat had come up with were still his best bet, from the gamblers like Rosenthal and Zelig up to the politicians like Waldo, Sullivan, and even Mayor William Gaynor.

One of them had something to hide, something that was worth *killing* to keep hidden, and he had to find out *what* it was in order to find out *who* it was.

After Runyon had sufficiently calmed the woman to the point where she could talk, he coaxed her address out of her, and asked her to contact them if she thought of anything else. That done, they decided it would be wiser for them to leave the park separately, and allowed her to go first.

"What do you think?" Runyon asked as they watched her walk away.

"I don't think she's lying, if that's what you mean. She has nothing to gain from it."

"Well," Runyon said, looking sheepish, "almost nothing . . ."

Bat looked at the younger man and asked, "How much did you give her?"

"Ten dollars."

"Uh-huh." Bat took out his wallet and offered Runyon five dollars.

Runyon didn't argue.

Once they were in the taxi headed back to Manhattan, Runyon said, "It's funny how you learn something new about people after they're dead."

"Yeah," Bat said, "funny."

After a moment Runyon said, "Are you going to tell Ida?"

"Hell, no. What's to be gained by doing that? Let the poor woman think her dead husband was faithful."

"Maybe he was," Runyon said, drawing a look from Bat. "I mean, maybe Inkspot and Milly were just friends."

Bat continued to stare at him.

"I mean, we forgot to ask exactly what was between them, didn't we?"

"No," Bat said, looking at the monuments in Grand Army Plaza. "I didn't *forget* to ask."

Although Bat had already decided not to tell Ida Jones about her husband's apparent transgressions, he didn't know until he got home that night that he wasn't going to tell his wife either.

It was late when he returned home from the Metropole, and Emma was going over Inkspot's papers, as she had taken to doing each night since Bat had removed them from Inkspot's desk.

"Emma—"

"Don't start in on me again, Bat," she said, looking up at him through tired eyes. "If all I can do to contribute is read these notes over and over again until something occurs to me, then that's what I want to do."

"You're a stuborn woman."

"No more or less stubborn than you."

"There is something else you could do, Emma."

"What?"

"You could continue to comfort Ida Jones."

"Ida is dealing with her loss much better than you might imagine, Bat," Emma said, sitting back in her chair, momentarily removing her attention from the papers spread out on the kitchen table. "She still has her memories."

Memories that he could take away from her at a moment's notice, he knew, if he told her what he had found out today.

"She still wants his killer caught, doesn't she?"

"I suppose so," Emma said, "but she doesn't really talk about it anymore, Bat. She really doesn't need me around trying to cater to her. I can do more good here."

"You might be right."

Emma frowned at him and asked, "Did you find out something today?"

"No," he said, rubbing his hands over his face. "I didn't find out anything."

"Bat Masterson," Emma said, standing up and crossing the room, "we've been married too long for you to try and pull that on me. What did you find out?"

He considered for a moment telling her, but that would only put her under the burden of trying to decide whether or not Ida should be told.

"You know that young Runyon and I have thought all along that Inkspot must have found out something that got him killed?" he said instead.

"What about it?"

"We also found out that it was definitely in some connection with Inkspot's job."

"Which means it should be in these notes," she said, indicating the mess on the table.

"I hate to ask you to keep reading them."

"Try asking me not to. If it's in there, I'll find it."

"I know you will, Emma. You're a pretty damned smart woman."

"How smart can I be, staying married to you for as long as I have?"

He smiled and said, "I've often wondered the same thing myself."

CHAPTER FIFTEEN

Since Runyon had run out of his office to find Bat with Milly Cabot's letter the day before, he had to pay for it the next morning by hitting the typewriter early.

Bat stopped in at his office simply to put in an appearance, but found Lieutenant Charles Becker waiting for him there.

"Charles, what a surprise."

"These your regular hours, Bat?" Becker asked. "Maybe I'm in the wrong racket."

"Been waiting long?"

"Only an hour."

"It's almost noon," Bat said, looking at his vest watch. "Must be important."

"It could be . . . to you."

"Tell me about it."

"Over lunch."

"All right."

"You buy."

"Give me a minute."

Bat stopped at his desk and, since he was vice-president, the early editions of most of New York's newspapers were there waiting for him, including the *Telegraph*. He looked a few of them over, hitting the high spots, and then stopped by Lewis's office to say he was going out.

"Out?" Lewis said, looking up from his desk. "You just got here."

"Business, Will. I've got a minion of the law waiting for me."

"Who?"

"Becker."

"Oh, him," Lewis said. "Listen, before you go, you got a message from City Hall."

"The mayor?"

"Yeah. You making friends or enemies?"

"What's the message?"

"The mayor won't be able to see you for a few more days," Lewis said. "Guess you're not making friends, huh?"

"No," Bat said. "I'm not the one who isn't making friends."

"I guess Gaynor doesn't want to see you."

"He'll see me, don't worry," Bat said, turning to leave.

"Did you see the item on page—" Lewis started to ask, but Bat knew what item he was talking about.

"I saw it."

"Trouble in paradise, eh?"

Did everyone know that Rosenthal and Becker were connected?

"I'll find out."

"That's the crime beat!"

"I'll turn it over to Malcolm when I get back, Will!"

They went to Shanley's, which meant that Bat was going to have to eat dinner somewhere else, but that decision would come later.

"All right," Bat said when they were set up at a table with lunch, "what's so important?"

"Bat," Becker said, looking extremely serious, "it's my own opinion that Herman Rosenthal killed Inkspot Jones."

Bat stopped short in the act of bringing his mug of beer to his mouth and said, "Where did that come from?"

"What do you mean?"

"Aren't you the one who was telling me as far back as October to stay out of it?"

"So, I've been thinking," Becker said with a shrug.

"Unofficially, of course."

"Of course."

"All right, then, why Rosenthal?" Bat asked. "Why not Kelly, or Zelig, or Monk Eastman?"

Becker shook his head and said, "Rosenthal."

"Is that your expert opinion?"

Becker nodded and said, "Unofficially."

Bat stared at Becker for a few moments, sipping beer and thinking over what the police lieutenant had just said.

It stunk.

Bat knew that Becker and Rosenthal were in bed together, and maybe the relationship was getting a little rocky.

"I saw in today's paper that Rosenthal's place got hit last night."

"That's right."

"That's kind of rare, isn't it?"

"We can't get to them all, Bat," Becker said, "but sooner or later . . ."

That was the article in the paper that Will Lewis had asked Bat if he'd seen, the one about Becker's strong-arm squad raiding Rosenthal's West Forty-fifth Street club. Apparently, Lewis knew about Becker's affiliation with Rosenthal, hence the "trouble in paradise" remark.

"And now you want me to believe that Rosenthal killed Inkspot," Bat said. "I thought we were friends, Charles."

"We are, Bat," Becker agreed, "which is why I've decided to help you find Inkspot's killer."

"And you suggest I start with Rosenthal?"

"I suggest that if you start with Rosenthal, you won't have to go much farther."

"All right, Charles," Bat said. "I'll keep your suggestion in mind."

Bat stood up, and Becker said, "Where are you going?"

"To the next name on my list."

"Which is?"

"Eastman."

"Monk?"

"Don't worry, I'll get to Rosenthal," Bat promised, "but I'm new at this detective business, so you've got to let me go about it my own way."

"Have it your own way," Lieutenant Becker said, "but there's one thing you really should know."

"What?"

"Today's Monk's day to go to the track."

"They're not racing at Belmont yet."

"That doesn't stop Monk," Becker said. "He owns a few horses and watches them work out."

"Thanks for the information, Charles," Bat said. "You saved me a trip to Chrystie Street."

"Like I said, Bat," Becker said, "I'm just trying to help."

"Finish your lunch," Bat said, "and I'll pay on my way out."

Bat found Monk Eastman by the Belmont training track, dressed much the way he dressed when he was at his Chrystie Street office: no jacket, no tie —and no shirt. He must have had skin like a polar bear.

Monk Eastman was a huge man, a street fighter whose past was written all over his face—scars, knots, cauliflower ears. Monk had fought his way to the top, and he still looked as if he could lick his weight in Five Pointers.

He was standing at the rail, watching a filly work out at six furlongs. As Bat approached, he saw a knife scar running across Eastman's muscular back down to his thick waist. He was not built muscularly with a trim waist, but rather like a tree trunk, the same thickness in his entire torso.

"One of yours?" Bat asked, coming up next to him.

It was cool out, but Eastman's upper torso was covered with sweat, and he didn't seem to feel the breeze.

"Who the hell are you?"

"My name's Bat Masterson, Monk. I'd like to talk to you about Inkspot Jones."

"I don't know what that is," Eastman said, keeping his eye on his filly. "What's an Inkspot Jones?"

"A newspaperman," Bat said. "A dead newspaperman."

"What's that got to do with me?" Eastman asked as his filly flashed past the finish line. "Damn," he said, "I could outrun that nag."

"I thought maybe you'd tell me what it had to do with you, Monk?"

Now that the horse had run her six furlongs, Eastman turned and glared down at Bat from his superior height. Bat felt an urge to back off, but steeled himself and did not.

"Look, you ain't a friend of mine, so you call me Mr. Eastman, right?"

"I'm not one of your boys, Monk."

"Maybe not," the big man said, "but I could break you in half as easy as I could any of them." He spread his feet for balance, took hold of Bat's upper arms, and squeezed, adding, "Easier, since you got older bones."

"This won't accomplish anything, Monk," Bat said, gritting his teeth against the pain. "I came here to talk to you."

"I don't usually see anybody without an appointment," Eastman said, squeezing tighter.

Perspiration broke out on Bat's forehead as Eastman increased the pressure on his arms, and he knew he'd have to do something before he cried out.

With a quick, snapping motion he brought his right knee up into Eastman's testicles, which were an easy target between the big man's wide-spread legs. Eastman grunted, and his eyes widened. His grip on Bat's arms weakened, and Bat pulled free and backed away, wincing as the blood began to circulate through his arms again.

"Damn you," Eastman said from between clenched teeth. "I'm gonna break your back."

The man took one step forward, but stopped when Bat produced the Peacemaker and pointed it at him. They stood that way for a few moments until Eastman licked his lips nervously and said, "Now, wait . . ."

"Now I know why they call you Monk," Bat said. "Because you've got the brains of a gorilla."

"I was just having some fun."

"Well, the fun's over, Monk. I came to talk, and that's what we're gonna do."

"Sure, sure," Eastman said. "I heard of you, you know. You used to be pretty good with a gun."

"I could hit you from this range with no problem."

Monk Eastman smiled nervously and said, "So let's talk."

"Did you know Inkspot Jones?"

"I heard of him. They fished him out of the Hudson, didn't they?"

"Before that," Bat said. "Did you know him before that?"

"I may have read his column or something," Eastman said, rubbing his injured testicles gently with his big right hand. "I follow sports."

"Look, Monk, let me say this right out. I'm looking for Inkspot Jones's killer, and if I find out it was you, or you had it done, I'll come back and show you just how good I am with a gun. You understand?"

"Sure, I understand. That's plain enough."

Movement on the track caught Bat's eye, and he saw that another horse had come out to be worked. "That one yours?"

Eastman looked at the track and said, "Yeah, he's mine."

"Any good?"

"He's a pig."

Bat backed off and, holstering the gun, said, "What else would you happen to own?"

Bat took the elevated back to Manhattan and headed straight for the Metropole. As he got off the train, his hands were still shaking, and he could feel the bruises blossoming on his upper arms. He needed a drink, but walked slowly to the Metropole, hoping that the shakes would be gone by the time he got there.

As he entered, he kept his hands in his pockets, but was forced to remove them when George Considine approached and held his out.

"Hello, Bat."

"George," Bat said. He withdrew one hand and, gratified to find it without even a quiver, grasped George's.

"Val's been waiting for you for over an hour."

"O'Farrell?"

"Yep. He told me what you've been up to," George said, looking at Bat with obvious admiration. "I think it's a fine thing you're doing, but I also think you're playing with fire. Be careful."

"I'm always careful, George," Bat said, but even as he said it he wondered how careful it had been to go and see a huge hulk like Monk Eastman alone.

Well, he *had* survived, hadn't he?

"Where's Val?"

"Back table. You look like you could use a beer. Anything wrong?"

Bat shook his head and said, "That damn elevated. Why don't they leave trains on the ground where they belong?"

"Progress."

Bat walked to the back and found Detective Val O'Farrell waiting there for him.

"Bat, have a seat."

"I understand you've been waiting for me," Bat said. "What's it about?"

"Have you seen Rosenthal yet?"

"No," Bat said, as Considine placed a cold beer in front of him and walked away. "I just came from seeing Eastman."

"And you saw Kelly yesterday."

"If you know that, then you also know who I saw before Kelly."

"I know," O'Farrell said. "I want to help you on this, Bat."

"This must be my lucky day," Bat said, sipping the beer gratefully. "Everybody wants to help me, especially two policemen."

"No, I really want to help you," O'Farrell said, "not like Becker. I think he's just looking to shake Rosenthal up a little more by sending you after him."

"From what I've heard about Rosenthal, it would take more than an old newspaperman to shake him up."

"Well, maybe Charlie Becker figures an old legend will do it."

"I doubt it. What have you got on your mind, Val?"

"I just wanted you to know that I want to help, Bat," O'Farrell said, "and I want to talk about it, but *after* you see Rosenthal."

"Why after?"

"Because you've gone about this the wrong way, Bat, but since you've started it you might as well talk to Herman like you talked to the others."

He would rather not talk to Rosenthal—or his man Kramer—the way he had just talked to Monk Eastman, but he kept that to himself.

"Meet me here tomorrow night and we'll talk."

"Why after Rosenthal?" Bat asked as O'Farrell rose to leave. "What about Jack Zelig? I've got to see him, too, don't I?"

"No, not Zelig," O'Farrell said with certainty.

"Why not?"

"He's the one man you can count out. What happened to Inkspot is just not Big Jack's style."

"Are you trying to tell me that Zelig doesn't kill people?"

O'Farrell shook his head slowly and said, "I'm telling you that if Zelig had killed Inkspot—or had him killed—he would have dumped his body in the middle of Longacre Square as a lesson to others." O'Farrell was one of those who had not yet begun to call Longacre Square by its new name, Times Square. He patted Bat on the shoulder and said, "Meet me here tomorrow night, Bat, and I'll tell you what you've been doing wrong."

CHAPTER SIXTEEN

The next day Bat and Runyon were sitting in Union Square Park, across the street from Rosenthal's Fourteenth Street restaurant. On the way there Bat had told Runyon what Becker and O'Farrell had told him.

"Two policemen trying to help, each in his own way, huh?"

"I guess."

"They're both friends of yours, Bat," Runyon pointed out. "Or supposed to be."

"They are."

"Then, what's going on?"

"Becker's after Rosenthal for some reason. O'Farrell—well, O'Farrell's funny. He might just want to help me, but if there's a chance that he can profit by it, he'll take it."

"What about Zelig?"

"All I know is what O'Farrell told me," Bat said, "and he might be right. I'll find out more tonight, I guess."

"Think he'll mind if I sit in?"

"He won't mind," Bat said, standing up as he saw the shade come up inside the restaurant window. "Time to go."

As they crossed the street, Bat asked, "Is the food any good here?"

"To tell you the truth," Runyon said, "I don't remember."

They went inside to a table, and as the waiter came out of the kitchen to greet the first diners of the day, he stopped short as he recognized Runyon.

"You," he said.

"Me," Runyon said, "and I've brought a friend."

"Do you want breakfast?"

"Why don't we skip the breakfast and get right to the point?" Bat said. "We'd like to see Rosenthal."

"Who should I say—"

"Tell him Bat Masterson is here."

The waiter nodded and left the room.

"Any minute he'll come back with Man-Mountain Kramer," Runyon said.

"You know," Bat said, aware of the dull ache in his upper arms, "I'd pay good money to see Kramer go up against Monk Eastman in the Garden."

"That would be interesting."

True to form, the waiter returned moments later with Kramer in tow.

"Masterson," Kramer said.

"Hello, Kramer."

They knew each other by sight.

"You can come up," the big man said, "but he'll have to stay here."

Runyon looked disappointed, but Bat told him, "You get to have breakfast."

"I just remembered," Runyon said.

"What?"

"The food here is terrible."

Bat and Kramer had nothing to say to each other as Bat followed the big man upstairs to Rosenthal's office.

"Bat Masterson," Kramer said after he'd opened the door. He stepped aside to allow Bat to enter. Rosenthal was seated behind his desk and made no move to get up or to shake hands.

"Well, I'm glad you came yourself this time," Rosenthal said.

"Have you heard from your friends, Rosenthal?" Bat asked. He moved to the center of the room and placed himself so that he could see both men. He wondered idly why Kramer had not searched him for a gun.

"What friends?"

"Kelly, Eastman, Sullivan—"

"They're no friends of mine. Why should I have heard from them?"

"I've already spoken to them about Inkspot Jones."

"So?"

"They seem to feel that you might have had a better motive to kill him, or to have him killed, than they would."

"Somebody's lying," Rosenthal said without missing a beat, "either you or them. It doesn't really matter, though. I don't know anything about that newspaperman's death, and that's the truth."

"The truth?" Bat said. "You wouldn't know the truth from a hill of beans, Rosenthal."

"I'm doing you a favor by seeing you, Masterson—" Rosenthal started, but Bat cut him off.

"You're seeing me for the same reason the others saw me," he said, "to make me think you've got nothing to hide. Well, I don't believe any of you."

"What you believe doesn't concern me."

"If that was true, I wouldn't be here."

"You're right about that," Rosenthal said. He looked at Kramer and said, "Remove Mr. Masterson."

Kramer grinned tightly and moved away from the door toward Bat. Bat had no intention of going through the same thing he'd gone through with Eastman the day before. He produced the Peacemaker right away and pointed it at Rosenthal. Kramer stopped short, and Rosenthal gaped.

"You let him in here with a gun?" Rosenthal demanded of Kramer in disbelief.

Kramer looked at his boss and, spreading his hands helplessly, said, "He's an old man. I didn't think he'd be carrying a gun."

"Well now, that was a real careless assumption on your part, Kramer," Bat said, interrupting them before they could continue.

"Put that thing away before I call a policeman," Rosenthal said, trying to brave it out.

"I've got a right to carry this weapon, Rosenthal. The police can't touch me—until I pull the trigger, of course."

"Which you won't."

"Not unless you or Kramer forces me to. You're not going to do that, are you, Kramer?"

"I'm going to break your neck," Kramer said angrily. Bat had embarrassed him in front of his boss, and in doing so had made an enemy for life.

"That's been tried by bigger men than you, Kramer," Bat said, "and recently. Now, be a good boy and shut up while I talk to your boss."

"Say your piece and get out," Rosenthal said.

"I'll tell you what I told the others, Herman," Bat said. "I'm going to keep looking until I find out who killed Inkspot Jones, and if it was you, I'll come after you."

"Did it ever occur to you that your friend might have deserved what he got?"

"Why? Because he found out something he shouldn't have and tried to turn it into cash?"

"How about this? How about maybe he just stuck his nose where it didn't belong?"

"Is that what you're saying happened, Rosenthal?"

"I'm not saying any such thing. I'm just giving you a for-instance or two."

"Whatever happened," he continued, "I'll find out, Herman. Be watching for me."

"You going to gun me down, the way you used to do it in the Old West, old man?" Rosenthal asked. "You better watch your own ass, Masterson."

"Send somebody after me, Herman," Bat said. "Go ahead. I'd love it. That'd be all the proof I need."

"I owe you for that fight fix, Masterson, and I always pay what I owe."

Bat turned the gun toward Kramer and said, "Move."

Kramer looked at Rosenthal for his orders, but Bat said quickly, "If he tells you to take it away from me, Kramer, will you do it? Do you think you could?"

Kramer looked at Bat, and then back at Rosenthal.

"Let him go," Rosenthal said in disgust.

Slowly, Kramer moved until he was standing alongside his boss's desk.

"I've had a real nice visit, gentlemen," Bat said, moving toward the door. "We may be doing this again soon."

"Don't bet on it," Rosenthal said.

Bat laughed, holstered the gun, and walked out. In the hall he was surprised at how rock-steady his hands were.

Maybe it was all coming back?

Or maybe he was too scared to shake.

"Let's go," he told Runyon, tapping his friend on the shoulder from behind.

Runyon jumped and said, "Jesus! What happened?"

"Let's talk about that outside," Bat said. He wanted to get out before
somebody got brave—or stupid.

Both newspapermen took care of the business they were getting paid to
take care of until they met at the Metropole that evening. Val O'Farrell had
not yet arrived, so both men had dinner and talked while they waited.

"Now that you've talked to all of them except Zelig," Runyon asked,
"what's your opinion?"

"My opinion?" Bat asked, laughing. "That I'm no detective. I feel like all
I'm doing is stumbling around in the dark."

"If you keep doing that," Runyon said with conviction, "sooner or later
you've got to bump into something."

"Yeah," Bat said, "like a bullet."

Runyon was about to reply when he saw Bat look past him and knew that
O'Farrell had arrived. Just at that moment he realized that Bat, out of old
habit, always sat so that he could see the door. He turned and saw O'Farrell
approaching their table.

"You're early," the detective said to Bat, sitting down between them and
laying his overcoat on the empty chair.

"So are you, which is just as well," Bat said. "We can get this over with
before any of the others arrive."

"Do you want Damon here to be in on this?" O'Farrell asked.

"He's my loyal assistant."

"Holmes and Watson," O'Farrell muttered.

"What?"

"Arthur Conan Doyle's detectives, Sherlock Holmes and Dr. Watson,"
Runyon explained.

"Don't know them."

"They're fictional," Runyon said. "Doyle is an English writer of detective
fiction."

"I'll catch up on my reading another time," Bat said. Looking at O'Farrell,
he said, "All right, Val, just what have I been doing wrong?"

"What have you been doing right?" O'Farrell asked.

"That's one I can't answer."

"Well, from what I can see and from what I've heard," O'Farrell said,
"you've managed to get quite a few people mad at you."

Frowning, Bat asked, "What have you heard, and from who?"

"*Who* I heard it from is the streets, Bat," O'Farrell said, "and I just told you *what* I heard. Since you started this investigation, all you've managed to do is make enemies."

"Like who?"

Ticking them off on his fingers, O'Farrell said, "Sullivan almost had a stroke, from what I heard, but we all know that he's got problems. Then there's Police Commissioner Waldo. You're not high on his list of people to invite to the next policemen's ball."

"That breaks my heart."

"It's not your heart I'm worried about," O'Farrell said. "It's your head. You've got Monk Eastman all worked up because you pointed a gun at him and kneed him in the balls."

"You did that?" Runyon asked, staring at Bat.

"It was either that or take a beating," Bat said with a shrug.

"You didn't tell me that," Runyon said, as if accusing Bat of withholding some juicy tidbit of information.

"Quiet," Bat said, "the man's talking." To O'Farrell he said, "You forgot Rosenthal and Kelly."

"Kelly's not mad at you," O'Farrell said. "In fact, in a way I think he admires what you're doing."

"Maybe he admires me so that I'll think it wasn't him who killed Inkspot."

"Maybe, but I don't think so."

"And Rosenthal?"

"Well, he was mad at you already, wasn't he? Over that fight fix? I don't think you endeared yourself to him with your visit."

"So in your expert opinion, both Kelly and Zelig had nothing to do with it."

"Right."

"That leaves Rosenthal and Eastman."

"And Sullivan, and Waldo—and Mayor Gaynor, who you haven't been able to get in to see—and a lot of other people in New York City."

"What are you telling me?" Bat asked. "That by concentrating on the biggest politicians and the biggest crime and gambling bosses in the city I made a mistake? That I've been wasting my time?"

"I don't think you've been wasting your time," O'Farrell said. "Look, you spoke with me before you started your murder investigation. Why don't you tell me everything you've been doing, and then I'll know better whether you've been wasting time or not."

"Sounds fair," Bat said and started talking, relating to O'Farrell everything he and Damon Runyon said and done and heard, and the conclusions he'd drawn.

The whole time Bat Masterson was talking, Val O'Farrell was sitting stock-still, listening intently. Runyon, looking at O'Farrell, could easily see what made the man such a good detective. He knew how to listen.

"All right," O'Farrell said, "all right. You've done better than I thought, Bat."

"Is that a compliment?" Bat asked. " 'Cause if it is, I don't feel like I deserve it."

"No, I'm serious," O'Farrell said. "You haven't done badly, you just started on the wrong foot."

"Well, don't keep me in suspense. Tell me which foot I *should* have started on."

CHAPTER SEVENTEEN

"You went after the right people, Bat," Val O'Farrell explained, "the people it made sense to go after, and that was right. But in doing that, you gave them a chance to clean their houses, and that was wrong."

"What do you mean?"

"I mean you let them know that you were coming, when what you should have done was dig and come at them from underneath."

"Wait a minute," Bat said, holding up his hands. Runyon could see the confusion on Bat's face, although he thought he knew what Val O'Farrell was getting at. "I'm just an old lawman from the West, Val. You have to explain this to me very carefully."

"It's easy, Bat," O'Farrell said, sitting forward. "Before you look for the man, you look for the motive. What you should have done was check into all of these people's business—quietly, of course—and see which of them might have had something worth killing Inkspot to keep quiet."

"That's easier for you to do than for me, Val. You've got the connections."

"You've got the connections, Bat."

"I don't—"

"You know Malcolm, don't you?"

"Malcolm?"

"Wood, Malcolm Wood," O'Farrell said. "The crime reporter for your paper?"

"Of course I know Malcolm."

"See? You do have contacts—Malcolm Wood's contacts."

"But Malcolm would have to be willing to let me talk to them."

"He's a newspaperman, isn't he? And it was a newspaperman who was killed. What was it Damon here wrote in his paper? Newspapermen are a close breed?"

"That's what I wrote."

"And what about your friends at the track, your gambling friends? Don't they know people who know people . . . ?"

"I suppose so."

"Then you've got contacts that you didn't even know about."

"All right, I see what you mean," Bat said. "I blundered."

"You didn't blunder, Bat," O'Farrell said. "You just made it a little harder to find out what you wanted. For the time being, stay away from Rosenthal and Kelly and Eastman and the others and concentrate on their businesses."

"Their business is gambling and crime and prostitution."

"Whatever it is, look into it," O'Farrell said, standing up. "I've got to get back to work, Bat."

"Wait a minute," Bat said. "What about Zelig? Should I check him out, too?"

"Why not?"

"You said you didn't think he had anything to do with it."

O'Farrell shrugged and said, "It wouldn't hurt to be thorough. Besides, Big Jack Zelig isn't long for this world anyway."

"What's that mean?"

"He'll be behind bars before the week is out. Your friend Becker will see to that."

"Becker's got something on Zelig?"

"Becker's got everything on Zelig," O'Farrell said, picking up his overcoat. "One more thing, Bat."

"What's that, Val?"

"When you check into the businesses of these men, don't forget that some of them are legitimate."

"Good point."

"Up to now you fellas have just been investigating," O'Farrell said. "It's going to be slow, methodical, hard, boring work, but now it's time for you to start doing some real *detecting*."

Emma Masterson sat back in her chair and rubbed her tired eyes. She had been over and over these notes, waiting for something to jump out at her, and it simply hadn't happened. She got up, made herself a fresh cup of tea, and then sat down to start all over again with the notes from the very first story that Inkspot Jones had worked on after arriving in New York.

The fire at the Polo Grounds . . .

"What do you think?" Damon Runyon asked after O'Farrell had gone.

Scowling, Bat said, "I think that I should probably have been led through this *investigation* by hand right from the beginning." The irony he put behind the word *investigation* was unmistakable.

"He did offer to help, then, didn't he?"

Bat nodded and said, "And I turned him down—out of pride."

"What about now?"

"Are you serious?" Bat asked. "To ask him to take part actively now would be like asking him to sign onto the crew of a sinking ship. I'm not going to ask him to come in and straighten out my mess."

"What are we going to do, then?"

"I'm going to follow his advice, of course," Bat said, "and use the contacts I didn't know I had—starting with Malcolm Wood."

"Will he go for it?"

"If I approach him the same way O'Farrell suggested, I think he will. Also, I may have to promise him the byline if and when we solve this case."

"Promise him yours," Runyon said, "but not mine."

"Don't worry," Bat said. "I don't make deals with something I don't own."

"I just wonder whose story people are going to read," Runyon said, "Malcolm Wood's or mine."

"They'll read both," Bat said, "but they'll like yours better."

"Why?"

"It'll be well written."

"Well, that doesn't really matter anyway," Runyon said, although he was obviously pleased by the compliment. "What matters is finding Inkspot's killer."

"That may be," Bat said, "but you can't bury that newsman's nose for a story, can you?"

"Can you?"

"I came to it in a roundabout way," Bat said. "I was a lot of things before I became a newsman—and I'm not even sure I'm one now."

"What are you, then?"

Bat thought it over for a few moments, then said, "A dinosaur."

When O'Farrell returned to police headquarters he started for his office but stopped short two steps past Lieutenant Charles Becker's. He thought it over for a moment, and then went in.

"Hello, Lieutenant," he said, standing just inside the doorway.

Becker looked up, saw O'Farrell, and frowned. The two men did not like each other.

"What do you want, O'Farrell?"

"I've just come from an interesting talk with a mutual friend."

"I didn't know we had any of those," Becker said, staring at the paperwork on his desk.

"Bat Masterson."

Becker's pen stopped moving and he looked up again, holding the pen in both hands. "What about Bat Masterson?"

"Nothing. I'm just giving him a hand with his investigation into Inkspot Jones's death."

"You have time to waste, O'Farrell?" Becker demanded. "If you do, I can see about getting you some more work."

"Don't pull rank on me, Becker," O'Farrell said. "Even if you have Waldo's ear, I'm the best detective this department has. That entitles me to a certain amount of freedom."

"Don't tempt me—"

"By the way," O'Farrell said, cutting Becker off, "how's your case against

Zelig going? You've been doing some pretty fine detective work yourself, as I hear it."

Becker knew damn well that O'Farrell was the best detective in the department, and he couldn't help but react to the compliment. "I've been doing all right," he said, shrugging modestly.

"But you've got enough to put him away?"

"He'll be gone by the end of the week."

"Why wait that long?"

"I—" Becker began, and then backed off. "That's my business, O'Farrell. Don't you have something to do?"

"Oh, I'm sure I could find something."

"Then find it. I'm busy."

Becker went back to his paperwork, and O'Farrell left to go back to his office. There was only one reason he could think of that Becker might be leaving Zelig free until the end of the week. The extra time would give Big Jack time to build an adequate defense against whatever Becker was going to hit him with—and that could mean only one thing.

A favor for a favor.

After O'Farrell left his office, Becker stood up, slipped on his jacket, and left the building. He had a meeting set with Rosenthal, to try to straighten out their differences. If that couldn't be done, then Becker had other plans, involving Big Jack Zelig.

Through a street source Becker had been feeding Zelig the information he needed to combat the case that was being built against him. It was important that Zelig know what he was up against so that he and his lawyers could figure out how to handle it. He *would* have to spend *some* time behind bars —that was unavoidable—but when he got out he'd remember that it was Becker who had made his shorter sentence possible.

Becker wondered, however, if it would ever occur to Zelig that it had also been he who had built the case against him in the first place.

Putting Zelig away, and then springing him, was all part of Becker's plan to put Zelig in his debt. If and when he called in that debt would depend entirely on Herman Rosenthal.

Of course, if Becker came up with his witness, he could put Zelig away for good. That would be a feather in his cap and might even be worth putting up with Rosenthal's crap a little bit longer.

Bat and Runyon spent some time at the Metropole waiting for either Tom O'Rourke or Tex Rickard to show up. Unfortunately, they never did. Neither did William Muldoon, who Bat thought might particularly be able to help them.

"Muldoon's got more boxing contacts than anyone I know," Bat explained to Runyon. "I wouldn't be surprised to see him become boxing commissioner somewhere on down the road."

"Well then, he's sure to know somebody that will be able to help us."

"And then there's Diamond Jim Brady," Bat said. "You know, I feel real dumb right about now. O'Farrell was right. I've got contacts I didn't even know I had, and I've been too dumb to realize it and use them."

"Speaking of which, will you talk to Malcolm Wood in the morning?"

"As soon as he gets into the office."

"You know, come to think of it," Runyon said, "I may have some contacts I don't know about either."

"Are you staying in town?"

"Yes."

"I've got an idea, then."

"What?"

"Why don't you come and stay with me tonight. Between us we can come up with a pretty good list of people to talk to."

"What about your wife?"

"She won't mind," Bat said. "She's as deeply involved in this as we are. She's convinced that she's going to find something in Inkspot's notes."

"If she doesn't go blind first."

"Well, we may be able to keep that from happening by getting home and helping her," Bat said.

"What are we waiting for?" Runyon asked. "It's time for this team to get some real detective work done."

"There's only one problem with that."

"What?"

Grinning ironically, Bat said, "This team wouldn't know real detective work if it up and bit us on the ass."

Section Four

Bat Masterson, Detective

The man who will back up what he says with a fight if necessary is to be respected.

—Bat Masterson, February 18, 1912
The New York Morning Telegraph

CHAPTER EIGHTEEN

Val O'Farrell had been right. It *was* hard, boring work, but Bat had taken the detective's advice to heart and was taking his time and doing it right.

And coming up empty.

Bat had approached Malcolm Wood first and had been surprised at how little persuading the man had needed to supply a few names of street people who might be able to help. Bat spoke to all of the people, who cooperated in deference to Malcolm Wood. Some of them flat out said they knew nothing, others said that they would keep their eyes and ears open—and *then* said they knew nothing.

After that, Bat had used Diamond Jim Brady, Tom O'Rourke, and William Muldoon as sources of contacts, none of whom were able to offer any information or even a guess as to who had killed Inkspot Jones.

Damon Runyon had tapped the crime reporter at his paper, as well as some gambling and sports friends of his own, but had come up with exactly the same results as Bat.

To say the least, it was a bit frustrating.

It was the first week of April when Bat and Runyon met at the Metropole to go over everything they had learned during the month gone by. Oh, they had seen enough of each other during that time, but this was the first time they were actually comparing notes, line by line, no matter how insignificant a fact might have seemed.

"They've all got legitimate business ventures," Runyon said, looking over his notes. Bat could see that Runyon's notes were written in a right, precise style, easy to read. His own notes were a conglomeration of cramped scribbles that were barely readable even to himself. Luckily, he had Emma, who had always been able to decipher her husband's "chicken scratches."

"To go along with their gambling and prostitution rackets."

Runyon nodded and continued. "Eastman owns racehorses—"

"If you can call that an honest racket."

"—Kelly's involved with a clothing manufacturer, if you can believe that—"

"I can."

"—and Rosenthal owns a construction company."

"Not a demolition company?"

Runyon pretended to squint at his notes and said, "Nope, it's a construction company. H&R Construction."

"All right," Bat said, consulting his own notes, some of which had been incorporated into Runyon's during their frequent exchanges of information. "Zelig's the only one without a legitimate enterprise."

"And he's still walking around free."

"I guess Becker didn't have as much on him as he thought."

"Well," Runyon said with a smirk, "this detecting business *is* a long and boring process."

"Tell me about it."

"All right then, for all our information what have we got?"

"Nothing that Inkspot should have been killed for knowing. None of the people we've spoken to—sports people, gambling people, or just plain street people—have been able to even hazard a guess."

"Or have been unwilling."

"The result is the same."

Runyon frowned and said, "Unfortunately, I agree. I can't see anything here worth killing him over."

"Damn it, there must be something!" Bat's vehemence was such that it attracted the attention of some of the other customers, and that of George Considine, who approached the table.

"If you two are going to have a spat, I wish you would do it someplace else."

"We're fine, George," Bat assured his friend, "although we could use another round of drinks."

"Trying to get ahead of the others, are you?" Considine asked, signaling the waiter at the same time. He was referring to Bat and Runyon's usual drinking cronies, who were still several hours away from their regular arrival time.

"Just trying to pass the time, George."

"Doing what? Arguing sports? Baseball? The season's just starting, isn't it?"

"It is," Runyon said.

"Then what's to argue about with such intensity that you have to disturb my other customers?"

"Murder," Bat said.

Considine opened his mouth to retort, then thought better of it. The waiter arrived with fresh beers, and after he had set them down and removed the empty mugs Considine said, "I appreciate your position, boys, but try and keep it down to a low roar, will you, please?"

"Sure, George," Bat said. "Don't worry about us."

"Easily said . . ." Considine replied, and went off to console his other patrons.

"We haven't heard from the woman in Brooklyn, have we?" Bat asked Runyon.

"No. Are we expecting to? She told us all she knew."

"Did she?"

"Didn't she?"

"I don't know."

"What would she have to hold back?" Runyon looked puzzled. "She didn't have to come forward in the first place, so why would she hold back?"

"I don't know," Bat said again, staring into his beer. "I just have a feeling we'll be hearing from her."

"Is your wife still going through Inkspot's papers?"

Bat laughed and said, "She's read some of them so often the ink is starting to fade, but at least she doesn't go at it every night anymore."

"Still think there's something in there none of us is seeing?"

Bat hesitated for a moment, then shook his head and said, "I don't know." He shook his head again and said disconsolately, "That's all I seem to be saying lately."

Runyon could see that frustration was really starting to set in on his friend, and he wished he could say something to cheer him up. Unfortunately, he, too, was starting to feel frustrated. They'd been "investigating" this thing to the best of their abilities for months, and still were unable to come up with something they could work with. Perhaps their best just wasn't good enough.

Bat drank some of his beer and then stood up.

"Not going to wait for the others?" Runyon asked.

"I'm sure they're sick of talking to me at this point," Bat said. He'd been pestering his friends over the past month, trying to use them as contacts—as Val O'Farrell had suggested—and trying to use *their* contacts as well.

"I think I'll try giving them a break tonight. Give them my best, will you?"

"I will. You take care, Bat. Get some rest."

"Sure, Al, sure. You, too."

As Bat left, they both knew that it would take more than rest to heal what ailed Bat Masterson.

Bat knew that his frustrations were starting to show through, and he knew that to a lesser degree, Damon Runyon was feeling it, too.

They had done everything Val O'Farrell suggested they do. They had stayed away from their prime suspects while investigating their backgrounds and businesses—legitimate and otherwise—but their efforts had gone unrewarded. In point of fact, Bat was somewhat surprised at just *how* legitimate some of their business had turned out to be. Apparently, the money they made from their illegal enterprises went toward building up their legal ones. Perhaps somewhere down the road their legitimate business would be doing so well that they'd abandon the gambling and the prostitution, the strong-arming and union busting.

Sure, and someday he and Wyatt Earp would make a motion picture today about their lives and times in the Old West.

When he arrived home, he was met at the door by Emma, who took his jacket.

"You're home early."

"Is that a complaint?"

"Not at all."

He removed the Colt from his belt and placed it on top of the chest of drawers. He had stopped wearing the shoulder rig he'd purchased and was starting to feel that it might be time to stop carrying the gun altogether.

He sat down heavily at the kitchen table and noticed that some of Inkspot's papers covered one side of it.

As Emma put a cup of coffee down in front of him, she said, "You look tired."

"Then I look like I feel?"

She put the coffeepot back on the stove and sat across from her husband. "Bat, I know this was my idea—"

"What was?"

"Your getting involved in this whole sordid mess of Inkspot's disappearance and death."

"No, it wasn't—"

"It was, partially," she argued, cutting him off. "It was I who urged you to get involved, for Ida's sake."

"And now?"

"And now for your sake I think you should drop the whole thing."

Bat leaned back in his chair with a puzzled look and asked, "Now, what's brought this on? Even when Damon and I were set upon by thugs—who probably had nothing to do with this mess, by the way—and I started carrying around that old Colt, you never suggested I quit. Why now?"

"Because you're going to make yourself ill," she said. "This past month you've been like a man possessed, getting up early, staying up until all hours, meeting with people of questionable morals in the vilest of neighborhoods."

"That doesn't sound so different from my everyday life, Emma."

"And you've dragged Damon along with you—only he's younger and can take the strain better."

"You're worried about my health?"

"I'm worried that you might be becoming obsessed."

Pointing at the papers that covered her portion of the table, he said, "You've got the nerve to call *me* obsessed?"

She looked down at the papers sheepishly and said, "Well, I'd finished my knitting . . ."

Bat sat forward and reached for Emma's hands, cradling them in his. "Look, old girl, this is something that I'm going to see through to the finish, even if it takes another year, and your young Mr. Runyon feels the same way I do. He doesn't need even an ounce of persuading on my part."

"No, of course not," Emma Masterson said softly.

"Now, why don't you rustle us up some dinner, eh? I'd like to get to bed early so I'll be fresh tomorrow."

She nodded and stood up, then turned back frowning and asked, "Fresh for what?"

"For whatever tomorrow may bring, dear lady," Bat said, "for whatever tomorrow may bring."

CHAPTER NINETEEN

The next day brought surprises, and none of them very pleasant.

When Bat arrived at work at the *Morning Telegraph*—some one and a half hours late—he found Damon Runyon waiting for him at his desk.

"Good morning. You get a job here, did you?"

"I found a letter waiting for me this morning when I got to work," Runyon said excitedly, standing up.

"From who?"

Runyon looked around and then said, "Milly Cabot."

"The lady from Brooklyn. What did she have to say?"

"Whatever it is, she wants to say it in person."

Bat scowled. "That means going out to Brooklyn again?"

"It does," Runyon said, "and this time she says to bring more than ten dollars."

Bat raised his eyebrows and said, "The lady thinks she has something to sell."

"Apparently."

"Then I guess we'd better go out to Brooklyn and hear what she has to say." Bat's tone was one of resignation.

"Obviously."

"Do you have an automobile waiting?"

"Definitely."

Bat nodded and said, "I thought you might."

Once again they drove over the Brooklyn Bridge, around Grand Army Plaza to the Botanical Gardens.

The gardens were in bloom, some flowers flaunting their colors fully, others still just blossoming, fifty acres of rainbow colors.

As they entered on foot, the cab having been told to wait, Bat asked, "The same place?"

Runyon nodded. "The children's garden."

They retraced their steps of months earlier and began looking about for Milly Cabot.

"I wonder what made her wait so long to get in touch?" Runyon asked.

"Maybe she wanted to see if we'd catch Inkspot's killer on our own."

"You think she might really have something to sell that will help?"

"I hope so." Bat's tone was *very* hopeful. "We haven't been doing all that great on our own, have we?"

Over near the children's garden there were two adult women with a group of small children, five or six years old, trailing along behind them. Obviously a school field trip of some sort. There was, however, no sign of Milly Cabot.

"Maybe she backed out," Runyon suggested.

"Maybe."

They milled about, waiting, watching the group of children. Bat noticed that one little girl had separated herself from the group, and watched with interest to see if she'd get lost, or if the adults would notice her absence. Eventually she got far enough away from the group to be in danger of being left behind, and as her class began to drift away, Bat moved toward her.

"What's wrong?" Runyon asked.

"Nothing."

The girl had disappeared behind some blossoming bushes, and as Bat reached them she suddenly came running out, slamming right into him.

"Whoa, hold on, Missy," he said, catching her by the arms.

"She's dead," the little girl said, looking up at Bat solemnly. "I got to tell my teacher."

"What are you talking about, girl?"

"The lady."

"What lady?"

"The one behind those bushes," the little girl said, pointing. "She's dead."

Bat suddenly felt a chill that shouldn't have been present with spring so near. "How do you know she's dead?"

"She looks like my aunt Sophie did when she died," the child said. "She's pale, like my aunt, but Aunt Sophie wasn't all bloody like this lady. Mister, I got to tell my teacher."

"All right," Bat said, releasing her arms. "Your class is over that way. You hurry so you won't get lost, and you tell your teacher."

"It's sad, isn't it, Mister?"

"What is?"

"That people have to die."

"Yes, Missy, it's very sad."

The little girl ran off to catch up to her class, and Runyon approached Bat, noticing the look on his face.

"What's wrong?"

"Either that's a fanciful little girl, or we've found Milly Cabot."

"Where?"

"Behind here."

Bat led the way behind the bushes, and it took them only scant second to find the woman. As the little girl had said, she was dead, lying there pale and bloody, her head at an odd angle because someone had almost sheared it off.

"Jesus," Runyon said. He grew as pale as the dead woman and fought to swallow back the contents of his stomach.

"We'll need some police, Al," Bat said, bending over the woman. "See if you can find any in the park."

"Is it—"

Bat smoothed the woman's hair away from her face, pulling some of it free from the blood it had adhered to.

"Yes, it's Milly Cabot."

"Jesus . . ."

"You asked me if I thought she'd have anything that we could use," Bat said, looking up at Damon Runyon. "I guess this answers that question, doesn't it?"

Runyon returned with a young patrolman in tow, who immediately lost his lunch. They waited for him to finish, then suggested that he call for some help. Eventually other patrolmen arrived, and then two detectives from the local police station.

"I know you," one detective said to Bat right away. "Bat Masterson, right?"

"That's right."

"And who's this?"

"Damon Runyon."

The other detective looked at Runyon and said, "I read your column."

"Thanks."

The first detective's name was Church, and the second Bannister. Church was a large, florid-faced man with a belly that hung over his belt. Bannister was tall and skinny. As far back as Bat could remember, fat men and skinny men always ended up as partners, for some reason.

Church stepped into the bushes to look at the body while Bannister stayed with Bat and Runyon.

"Who found her?"

"A little girl who was here with a school field trip or something," Bat said. "One of your patrolmen has already talked to her and gotten her name."

Bannister turned to look at the patrolman in question, who nodded. "How do you two happen to be here? There's no sports to cover here."

"We got an urge to look at some flowers," Bat said.

"Very funny."

"What's funny?" Church asked, returning to his partner's side.

"These fellas happened to be here looking at the flowers."

"Is that so?"

"No, it's not," Bat said, and then went on to explain why he and Runyon were there. There was more to be lost than gained by not cooperating, and there was really no reason not to.

"You're working on a murder case?" Church asked.

"That's right."

"You got some, uh, official standing?"

Bat showed him the Pinkerton I.D.

"And him?" Church indicated Runyon as he handed the I.D. back.

"He just came along for the ride."

"How'd you get here?"

Bat made a face and said, "Automobile."

"Wave of the future," Church said solemnly. "Anybody talk to your driver?"

"You'll have to ask your boys that."

Church looked at Bannister, who nodded and went off to take care of it. At that point another man arrived, carrying a black doctor's bag.

"Coroner," Church said. "In the bushes, Doc." He looked back at Bat and Runyon and said, "You two won't mind sticking around for a while?"

"As long as you need us," Bat said.

"That's nice of you. Just stand off to one side, will you?"

Bat and Runyon moved out of the way and watched while the coroner went about his business and then had the body removed. During that time Bannister returned, and both he and his partner conferred with the doctor and the patrolman who had taken the little girl's statement.

"How long do you think they'll keep us?" Runyon asked.

"Not much longer. They'll get all the stories, match them up, and then let us go."

"Ah, what's the difference anyway?" Runyon was disgusted. "We've got no place else to go. Whatever Milly Cabot knew died with her, and that leaves us facing a blank wall again."

"Not necessarily."

"What do you mean?"

"We've got a new development now, and something new may come out of this. You never know."

Church and Bannister approached them, and Bat and Runyon moved forward to meet them.

"Do you think that this murder and the killing of your friend are connected?" Church asked Bat.

"It seems reasonable to me."

"What did her note to you say, Mr. Runyon?"

"Just that she had some information we might need, and that we should bring money."

Church looked up at his taller partner and scratched the side of his nose. "You know what I think?"

"What?"

"I think she tried to sell her information to somebody else first, and when they wouldn't go for it, she sent you that note."

"That seems reasonable, too," Bat agreed.

"Sure it does." Church looked pleased with the turn of events. "Whoever else she tried to sell it to decided to save his money and just kill her. Yep, I think the two killings are connected, all right, and that means I can toss this one into Manhattan's lap and let them handle both of them."

"I'm sure Lieutenant Becker will be glad to hear that," Bat said.

"Charlie Becker?" Bannister asked.

"You know him?"

"I heard of him. Commissioner's man, ain't he?" The policeman's tone made clear what he thought about a cop who would be the "commissioner's man."

"I suppose."

Both men now looked pleased at having something they could drop into Becker's lap.

"Well then, that wraps this one up," Church said, rubbing his hands together. "We'll just send our reports up to Lieutenant Becker."

"Can we go?" Bat asked.

"Sure. Your story checks out. Your driver is still waiting for you at the front entrance."

"Thanks."

As he and Runyon turned to leave, Bat heard what sounded like one detective slapping the other one on the back.

"Another one wrapped up," he said beneath his breath to Runyon. "A dedicated police department at work."

The ride back to Manhattan was a quiet one, each man lost in his own thoughts.

Despite what he had said about Milly Cabot's murder being a "new development" out of which something useful might come, Bat was depressed. The message from the woman had given him some hope of finding out something new, something that might eventually—finally—lead them to Inkspot's killer. Now all they had was another murder. He looked over at Damon Runyon, who was staring straight ahead, and wondered what was on the younger man's mind.

As if responding to Bat's mental question, Runyon's eyes suddenly focused and he turned to Bat and asked, "Are we going to work on this one, too?"

"The great detective team work on another case? We can't even solve one. We're going to try two?"

"Are we going to ignore it, then?"

"No, we can't ignore it. It can't possibly be a coincidence. I'll have a talk with Becker and see if he won't keep me up to date on his progress."

"Will you talk with him today?"

"Oh, no." Bat shook his head firmly. "Today he'll be hearing the good news that he's getting another homicide to solve. He won't be fit company for man nor beast, not today. I'll have a talk with him tomorrow."

"And what do we do with the rest of today?"

"We've got regular jobs to tend to, lad." Bat slapped Runyon on the back soundly and added, "Let's get to them."

CHAPTER TWENTY

"Have I thanked you for having this dumped in my lap?" Lieutenant Charles Becker asked.

Bat had waited judiciously—he thought—until the afternoon to go to Becker's office to talk with him. He had been there all of ten minutes, and this was the third time Becker had sarcastically voiced his gratitude.

"Charles, I didn't tell those other detectives to drop this on you."

"No, but you were pretty quick with my name, weren't you?"

"They asked me who the best policeman in New York was. Could I lie?"

"Hogwash!"

Bat couldn't argue that, so he remained silent.

"Now that I've got this case as well as the other, what is it you want?"

"I only want you to let me know what progress you make on the Milly Cabot case, as regards the Inkspot Jones case."

Becker was frowning mightily, and Bat knew why. The Inkspot Jones case had been unofficially closed for some time, he knew. Now that the woman, Milly Cabot, a known associate of Inkspot Jones's—thanks to Bat's information—had been killed, Becker would be forced to resurrect Inkspot's case and coordinate both.

Becker said, "Are you still working on the Jones case?"

"Yes."

"Still carrying that Pink I.D.?"

"Yes."

"Bat—" Becker began, but he stopped himself short when he realized how fruitless his intended words would be. Instead he said, "Stay out of the way and I'll see what I can do about passing you information."

"I appreciate this, Charles."

"I'm sure."

"By the way, just out of curiosity, how's your case against Zelig going?"

Scowling, Becker replied, "Don't ask."

When no further explanation was forthcoming, Bat decided to let the question lie. He could always ask Malcolm Wood what he knew about it.

He stood up and said, "I'll stand you to the best dinner of your life when this is all over, Charles."

"Sure," Becker said. "By then I'll not have the teeth to eat oatmeal with."

On his way to the door Bat said, "But it will be the finest oatmeal money can buy!"

After Bat left, Becker continued to scowl at the wall opposite his desk. His case against Zelig had dissipated when his prize witness had shown up dead. The papers had not covered the man's death very thoroughly, because on his own he was insignificant. Only Becker had known how important a role the man would play in putting Zelig away for good—or so he had thought. The man's brutal murder had proven otherwise, and now Becker was almost back to where he'd begun. He could still put Zelig behind bars, but not for nearly as long as he had thought.

And now he had this to contend with, as well as a growing dissatisfaction with his arrangement with Herman Rosenthal.

Things were starting to pile up on him, and what he hadn't needed was another goddamned murder to work on.

That meal that Bat Masterson had promised him was going to have to be a feast to make up for this!

Runyon had been unable to accompany Bat to his meeting with Becker, but was waiting for him that evening at the Metropole.

"Where are the others?" Bat asked, joining Runyon at a table.

"No one's arrived yet."

"You know, I've often thought we should give this little gathering a name of some sort. You know, like The Sportsmen's Club or something?"

"How about The Liar's Club?"

Bat frowned and said, "Let's address that question at another time."

He caught a waiter's eye and signaled for two beers to be brought over, in spite of the fact that Runyon's glass was only half empty.

"I'm still working on this one," Runyon said, raising his glass.

"They're both for me," Bat informed him, and Runyon grinned.

"Well, did you see Becker?"

"I did."

"And?"

"He is not a happy man."

"But?"

"But he'll keep me informed."

"And will he?"

Bat hesitated a moment, then said, "I think he will. He has other fish to catch."

"Meaning Zelig?"

Bat nodded and continued. "I think he'd welcome any help in closing the cases of the deaths of Inkspot and Milly Cabot."

"I hope so. *I'd* certainly welcome some."

The waiter came with the beers, and Bat gratefully consumed half of one.

"What's happened to Becker's case against Zelig?"

"I asked him that question myself and got no answer, so I went to Malcolm Wood."

"And?"

"It seems Becker had himself a prime witness against Zelig, but the man's name was not as much of a secret as the good lieutenant thought."

"And he turned up dead."

"Right."

"How much attention do you think he'll really pay to the murder of some woman in Brooklyn when he's got Big Jack Zelig to go after?"

"I don't know. I guess that remains to be seen, doesn't it?"

At that point both Muldoon and O'Rourke arrived, with tidings that both Lewis brothers and Tex Rickard would soon be joining them. Upon *their* arrival the beer and liquor began to flow steadily, and eventually Bat again brought up his suggestion of naming their small nightly gathering.

"How about The Liar's Club?" Runyon suggested, and the others graced him with stares and glares that could only have been politely described as baleful.

As the remains of the as yet unnamed group began to break up late that night, Val O'Farrell—the only one of their number who had been missing— entered and approached the table at which only Bat was still seated. Damon Runyon had been the first to leave, and at that moment Tex Rickard was on his feet, preparing to leave Bat alone.

"Ah," Rickard said, spotting O'Farrell, "you are saved from having your last drink of the night alone, and I from the guilt of leaving you to it."

"Go, and take your guilt with you."

Rickard bade good night to O'Farrell as they passed.

"Time for another drink?" the detective asked, taking the seat just vacated by Rickard.

"Always," Bat said, signaling the waiter. "And what kept you from joining us until this late hour?"

"What else but work would detain me?"

"Or a pretty lady."

O'Farrell smiled wistfully and said, "That, too." The detective accepted the beer from the waiter and sipped from it gratefully. "Ahhh." He set the brew down carefully on the table before him. Sitting back in his seat, lacing his fingers together over a slight paunch, he said, "Tell me, how goes your investigation?"

"Not well." Bat thought he might have sounded a bit petulant, but was pleased that he was apparently still a drink or two shy of moroseness.

"Tell me," O'Farrell said, and it was all the coaxing Bat needed.

Gratefully, Bat began to talk. When the story was done, O'Farrell again sipped his beer and then said, "I heard about the woman, but I didn't know you were involved. Your friend Becker was ranting about it every chance he got."

"I wonder what she would have told us if we'd reached her in time." Bat apparently had not heard O'Farrell's last remark, for he had a faraway look in his eyes.

"I hesitate to mention this," O'Farrell said gently, "as I understand your considerable dislike for automobiles and would never dare suggest that you go back to Brooklyn in one, but . . ."

"But what?"

"Have you checked the woman's home?"

"We—" He had been about to say that they had never thought of it, but even he realized how foolish that would sound. So he covered by saying, "I don't think we could get in. After all, it is the home of a murder victim. We'd need permission."

"You won't need permission. It's the victim's home, but it is not a crime scene. *How* you get in, however, would be up to you."

"Which would necessitate another trip to Brooklyn."

"I would never even suggest—"

"Never mind," Bat said, waving a hand and cutting him off. "If I'd been smart enough to think of it while we were already out there . . ."

"We can't all be great detectives," O'Farrell said, grinning.

"No," Bat said, standing up and looking down at his friend, "but some of us are lucky enough to have one as a friend."

"You embarrass me."

"I thank you," Bat corrected him. "The other I leave to you alone to accomplish. Lord knows, I could probably give you lessons, but the hour is late."

CHAPTER TWENTY-ONE

Milly Cabot had lived in an apartment in a house on Eighth Avenue, in the Park Slope section of Brooklyn, not far from the Botanical Gardens.

As Val O'Farrell had promised, there was no official seal on the front door.

"How do we get in?" Runyon asked.

"How else?"

They knocked on the front door, and the landlord who appeared was an elderly man in his sixties. Thinking this, Bat then realized how close to sixty he was himself. Was he the elderly? He shook the thought off and promptly bribed the man to let them into Milly's apartment.

"It was a shame about Milly," the man said, leading them to the second floor. "A shame."

He opened the door with his key and then, as he began to enter behind them, Bat put his hand against the man's frail chest.

"I shouldn't let you in there alone," the landlord protested.

"For ten dollars you should rent it to me for the month. We'll lock up when we're through."

The man reluctantly backed away, and Bat closed the door in his face.

"Now what?" Runyon asked.

"We look around."

"For what?"

"If I knew that, then we wouldn't have to look around. Maybe Inkspot left something with her for safekeeping."

Runyon brightened and said, "Maybe that's what she wanted to sell us?"

"Then let's look."

The apartment seems clean enough, although it could have been neater. The pillows on the couch, for instance, were askew, the books on the bookshelf were turned every which way, and the drawers of the small wooden desk were ajar. And the top of the desk—

"I think we're too late," Bat said suddenly, looking around him.

"What makes you say that?"

"Milly Cabot seemed to me to be a fairly well dressed, well kept woman. Does this look like the apartment of a well-kept woman?"

Runyon looked about and then said to Bat, "So it's a little sloppy."

"It's not a little sloppy, my friend. It's already been searched."

Runyon looked around again quickly, as if someone might still be there.

"They're gone, but they did a thorough job. If there was anything to find, they probably found it."

"Aw, damn—"

"Unless it wasn't here to begin with."

"Well, if it's not in the papers we took off Inkspot's desk and it's not here, where is it?"

"I don't know, but while we're here we might as well finish looking around."

"Seems pretty futile to me," Runyon muttered, but again they set about their task, with considerably less optimism than before.

After half an hour Bat said, "Well, that's it, then. There's nothing here." Runyon was over by a bookcase, shoving books aside and looking behind them.

"What's that?" Bat asked suddenly.

"What?"

"That, near your right hand."

Runyon frowned, squinted, then slid a book off the shelf and said, "This?"

"Yes."

Bat strode across the room and took the book from Runyon's hand. It was a copy of *The Sunset Trail* by Alfred Henry Lewis. Published in 1905, this book by Bat's friend purported to be the true story of the legend that was Bat Masterson.

"Surely you've read that—" Runyon began.

"Is it a coincidence that it's here?" Bat asked, cutting him off.

"Why not? Lots of people have read it."

"Not so many," Bat said wryly. "No, I think perhaps Inkspot left this here, and maybe . . ."

Bat began to leaf through the pages, then impatiently turned the book upside down in his hand and fanned the pages, so that anything that might be hidden inside would fall to the floor.

And fall it did, sliding from between the pages and fluttering downward like a drunken butterfly.

"What is it?"

"Let me catch it and I'll tell you."

Bat Masterson's right hand, once legendary for its quickness, reached twice and missed. He set the book down and patiently waited for the slip of paper to light before picking it up off the floor.

"It's a newspaper article," he said, frowning at it.

"From what paper?"

"The *Telegraph*."

"And what's it about?"

Runyon crowded closer so he could see over Bat's shoulder. They both read the bold-print legend that declared, POLO GROUNDS BURN DOWN. It was a two-paragraph piece describing the fire, and the byline was "Delaney Jones."

The date was April of the previous year, the month Inkspot Jones arrived in New York.

"A bookmark?" Runyon asked.

"Possibly, but I still don't think the book was here by coincidence."

"But what good could this possibly do—" Runyon started, and then changed his tune. "Surely a newspaper article isn't reason enough to kill a woman over."

Bat spread his hands helplessly and said, "It's all we've found, isn't it?"

"Well . . ."

"Have you fanned through these other books?"

"No, but—"

"Let's do it, then."

They removed the thirty or forty books from the shelves and fanned through them the way Bat had fanned *The Sunset Trail*, yielding nothing but an occasional blank piece of paper that had obviously been used as a bookmark.

"There, then," Bat said, placing the last of the books back on the shelf.

"There . . . what?" Runyon's puzzlement was plainly evident. "We found nothing."

"We found her bookmarks. She preferred to use blank paper, so this article was not a bookmark. It was put in that book for an entirely different purpose."

"To hide it?"

"I'd guess yes. It could have been her, or Inkspot could have asked her to hold the book without telling her what was in it. But whatever the case, I don't believe it was there by accident."

"What do we do now?"

"We lock up and go back to my apartment," Bat said, hurriedly tucking the article into his vest pocket. "I want another look through Inkspot's papers."

Emma Masterson was surprised by the appearance of her husband and Damon Runyon in the middle of the day.

"What's going on?" she asked as they rushed into the apartment, obviously agitated over something.

"Where are Inkspot's papers, Emma?"

"In the top drawer. I was going to look at them again tonight."

"You may not have to," Bat said, moving toward the dresser and sliding open the top drawer. Without taking the papers out, he began to leaf through them.

"If you tell me what you're looking for, maybe I can help you," Emma said, moving alongside her husband. "I practically know them by heart."

"I'm looking for this," he said, removing the article from his pocket and showing it to her.

"That? That's easy, it was the first thing he worked on when he got here."

Bat moved aside to allow her access to the drawer, and she produced Inkspot's original of the article in seconds.

"That's it."

Bat took it, read it quickly, and then handed it to Runyon.

"It's no different from the article in print," Runyon said after he'd read it.

"Did you expect it to be?" Emma asked them both.

"We don't know what we expected, Emma," Bat said, taking the paper back from Runyon. There was some scribbling in the margins, and he tried to read that now.

"Emma, can you—"

"Here, let me," she said, taking it from him. "There are a few notations, but most of them are in pencil, and they're almost all smudged. Here's one that says . . . it says 'accident.' "

"What's that?" Bat asked, pointing to the word.

"It looks like a question mark after the word."

"So it doesn't say 'accident,' " Bat reasoned. "It's asking 'accident?' "

"I suppose so, yes."

"But the article *says* the fire was an accident," Runyon said.

"No, it doesn't, lad," Bat said. "You've got to read it more carefully. It says that the *fire department* says the fire was an accident."

"What's the difference?"

"I'll tell you what the difference is," Bat said, taking the paper from his wife. "If Delaney Jones thought the fire *wasn't* an accident, he'd go out and try to prove it."

"Are you saying—"

"I'm saying maybe he did just that. Maybe he went out, found out that the fire had been set, found out by whom, and instead of turning it into a story, decided to try and turn it into a lot of money." Bat held the article up triumphantly and said, "I think we're looking at the reason Delaney Jones was killed!"

CHAPTER TWENTY-TWO

"That's fine," Damon Runyon said. "We may know *why* Inkspot was killed, and *how*, but we still don't know by *who*."

"This is a start in the right direction," Bat said, excitedly, but he noticed that Runyon wasn't sharing his enthusiasm. "What's wrong?"

"I'm just wondering if we're not reading too much into one small article."

"You need proof, huh?"

"Wouldn't the police?"

"All right, then we'll get proof."

"How?"

"We'll investigate the fire."

Runyon's eyes went skyward. "We're already investigating two murders, one that's months old, and now you want to take on a possible arson that's over a year old? We haven't been doing all that well as it is, Bat."

"What other choice do we have?" Bat asked, holding the article out. "This is all we have to go on, Al. If we don't follow it up, we might as well fold up our tents. Are you willing to do that?"

Runyon's jaw stiffened, and he said, "I'll go with it as long as you will, Bat. You know that."

"I know it, Al," Bat said, putting a hand on Runyon's shoulder and squeezing.

"How do we go about investigating this fire, then?"

"The first thing we'll do is each check out the morgues at our own newspapers. Reach everything you can find on the fire, and then meet me at the Metropole this evening and we'll compare notes."

"I've also got a column to write today."

"And so do I. All the more reason why we should get started right now."

Bat kissed Emma on the cheek and told her to put Inkspot's papers away. "We may just be able to give them to Ida very soon."

"I hope so," Emma said.

Bat and Runyon left and stopped down on the street before splitting up.

"Bat, are you going to let Becker in on this?"

Bat thought it over for a moment, then said, "I don't think so. I admit I got pretty worked up over this, Al, but you were right. There's no proof, and that's what Becker would need to take it seriously."

"Well then, let's go and find some."

"I'm with you, lad."

They split up at that point, each going to his respective paper to get his column done so they could spend as much time as possible in the morgue, where all the old issues were kept.

To get himself into the mood, Bat devoted his column to the fledgling baseball season and the Giants' chances to win the Pennant. Then he retired to the *Telegraph*'s morgue, which was in the building's basement.

The morgue was ruled by one Andy Sheffield, an ex-reporter in his eighties who was now content to sit in charge of all of the *Telegraph*'s old news. Bat knew Andy, and made a small stop before going downstairs.

"How're you doing, Andy?"

The old man looked up from his desk top and squinted his rheumy eyes to see who was speaking. "Is that Masterson, the living legend?"

"It's Masterson," Bat said, "but that's all I'll admit to."

"What's a big shot vice-president like you doing down here among the ruins?" Sheffield always said that the old newspapers reflected the ruins of the past, and that it was fitting that an old ruin like him should be put in charge.

"I brought you a present, Andy," Bat said, and from behind his back he produced a bottle of fine cognac.

Sheffield regarded the bottle warily as it dangled from Bat's hand by the neck and said, "And what do I have to do for it?"

"Just let me rummage around down here for a while, that's all."

"How long?"

"Can't say. As long as it takes, I guess."

"Won't make a mess, will you?"

"I promise not to. Have we got a deal?"

Bat dangled the bottle closer to the old man, who finally snatched it from his hand with a triumphant "Done!"

Sheffield busied himself with the cognac while Bat went in among the many shelves and drawers of old newsprint.

He quickly discovered that a person could get lost wading through the past as he read articles not only on the fire but on the baseball season of that year in general. While he was down there he also started to read the various stories that had been printed during the year about Rosenthal, Kelly, Eastman, and Zelig, all of which made interesting reading.

As for the fire, it had occurred early in the season, forcing the Giants into sharing Highlander Park with New York's other team, the Yankees. There was no mention of an investigation into the cause of the fire, but neither was there mention of any reason to suspect that it might not have been accidental. The articles were equally vague—or evasive—on just what had caused the fire.

So the first thing they had to find out was the exact cause of the fire, and from there they could ascertain whether or not it was deliberately set.

When Bat left the morgue his hands were black with dust and newsprint, and he was surprised to see that several hours had gone by. Old Man Sheffield was dozing with his head down on the desk, the empty cognac bottle close at hand. Bat left and locked the door behind him.

Going back upstairs, he thought that he had the beginnings of a theory in the works—but he was determined that he would keep it to himself until he had it completely figured out.

He wondered how Damon Runyon was doing.

Back upstairs, Bat realized how late it was when he saw how many people had gone home. In the act of leaving was Malcolm Wood, and Bat quickly intercepted him.

"I'm not giving away any more of my sources, Bat," Wood said, and Bat could see that he was only partially kidding.

"I'm not going to ask you, Malcolm."

"What can I do for you, then?"

"Do you remember the fire at the Polo Grounds last year?"

"Sure I do, why?"

"What did you hear about it?"

Wood frowned and asked, "What specifically are you looking for, Bat?"

"Was there any mention of it having been set?"

"You mean deliberately?"

Bat nodded.

"Not that I heard, but then it was really handled by the sports side—hey, wait a minute. Inkspot handled that story, didn't he?"

"Yes, but his material is pretty vague about how the fire started."

"Has this got something to do with his death?"

Bat backed up a bit, not wanting to give away his lead to Wood. "I don't know, Malcolm. I'm just checking out the stories Inkspot worked on since his arrival, and that was his first."

That seemed to satisfy the crime reporter.

"Well, I didn't hear anything about it being set on purpose."

"Did you hear anything about it *not* being set on purpose?"

"No, come to think of it, I didn't. I guess that was pretty vague, wasn't it?"

"That's the way it seems to me. Thanks for your help, Malcolm."

"If I remember correctly—" Malcolm Wood started as Bat was walking away. Bat stopped and turned back, waiting for Wood to continue. "If I remember correctly, the crime side did get into that later on, although it wasn't me."

"What was that about?"

"Seems a workman was killed in that fire. His body wasn't discovered until later, when they started cleaning the place up."

"I don't remember that."

"I do, now that you brought the whole thing up again. That means if the fire *was* set on purpose, then whoever set it is guilty of murder."

And that, Bat thought as Wood took his leave, would be the motive someone would have needed to kill Delaney Jones.

Bat was at his desk wondering if he should go back down to the morgue to look up the story on the dead workman when William Lewis came out of his office.

"Well, it's nice to see you putting in some late hours, Mr. Vice-President."

"William, do you remember the fire at the Polo Grounds last year?"

"Sure I do. Everyone thought the Giants' season would suffer playing in a strange park, but they were—"

"Do you remember sending Inkspot out on that story?"

Lewis thought a moment and then said, "Yeah, I think that was his first story, wasn't it?"

"It was. William, where was I? I can't seem to remember."

"Well, I rarely know where you are, Bat, but as I recall, you were at the track. Once I sent Inkspot out on it, I had to leave the story in his hands."

Bat nodded his understanding of that, but frowned as he tried to remember the period of the incident last year. I must be getting old, he thought. My memory is going.

"Does this have something to do with Delaney Jones's death? Are you still working on that?"

"I'm just checking up on some of his stories," Bat said, giving Lewis the same explanation that he'd given Malcolm Wood.

"Uh-huh. You gonna stay around or come over to the Metropole?"

"I've got to meet Damon Runyon at the Metropole."

"Well, I'll let the boys know that you're coming, but the way you look, I don't know if you'll be very good company tonight."

"Thanks, William," Bat said absently. "Good night to you, too."

Lewis stared at Bat Masterson for a moment, then shook his head slowly and left the office.

Bat remained there for another hour, adding the news of the dead workman to the theory he'd started to formulate in the basement.

He no longer had any doubt but that Inkspot was killed because he had found out about the arson, poked around, and discovered who had set the fire, killing the workman. Now, Bat would never have thought Inkspot capable of blackmail, but there were a lot of friends in Bat Masterson's past who had done things out of character. In addition to the blackmail there was the "affair"—such as it might have been—with Milly Cabot. Again, that was something Bat would never have suspected Inkspot Jones of.

The theory was fine, having the motive was a step in the right direction, but finding out who was the man behind the arson and the killings was something else again. In fact, it was what he and Damon Runyon had already spent months trying to do, without success.

Runyon had been right to control his reaction to the newspaper article.

They knew how and they knew why, but they didn't know the all-important *who*, and although they knew more now than they had before, they were still a long way away from solving that.

Bat had several options. He could go to Becker with what he'd found out, or he could go to O'Farrell and ask the man for more help.

The other option was to do what Inkspot had done: retrace the steps *he* had taken when he suddenly stumbled onto the information that got him killed.

Bat had been away from the office when the fire had first occurred, or he would have covered the story then. Now, a year later, he was going to cover it the way Inkspot had covered it with—he hoped—different results.

By the time Bat reached the Metropole, Damon Runyon was sitting alone, nursing his last beer of the night. He looked up as Bat sat down and said, "I almost gave up on you."

"Where are the others?"

"Left, for one reason or another."

"Was O'Farrell here?"

"No, he was working on something. William said you were in the office, working."

Bat signaled the waiter for a beer and said, "I was thinking."

"About what?"

"About what I found out tonight," Bat said, and went on to explain to Runyon everything he'd read and heard. He did not, however, propose his theory to his young friend. He was not ready for that yet.

"That all jibes with what I found out," Runyon said, digging into his jacket pocket. "Only I *did* come up with something on the death of the workman."

It was a small piece, smaller even than the one they'd found in Milly Cabot's apartment. WORKMAN KILLED IN POLO GROUNDS BLAZE the bold print said, and the short paragraph went on to explain that during the cleanup of the charred ruin, the body of a workman had been found and later identified as one Sam Peterson. Nobody seemed to know what Peterson was doing there, but it was established that he was a worker at the park, kept on staff to effect small repairs.

"I wonder what kind of small repairs he was effecting when the fire started," Bat said, handing back the article.

"In the middle of the night?"

Bat nodded. "Exactly. It would make more sense if this Peterson character was there setting the fire himself."

"And got trapped in his own blaze?"

"It's something else we're going to have to look into."

"Look, Bat, why don't we divvy up the work? You check out the fire and I'll check into this fella's background. If we can establish a link between him and Zelig or one of the others, we'll have our man."

"Good thinking, lad," Bat said. "First thing in the morning we'll each embark on our allotted tasks, and rendezvous here to compare notes."

"We should rent a booth from George and hang out a shingle," Runyon suggested. "Runyon & Masterson, Investigators."

"Masterson & Runyon," Bat said. "But either way I don't think George would like it."

They finished their beers, bade good night to George Considine, and stopped outside for one last exchange.

"Look, lad, maybe we should change jobs."

"Oh, no, it's all been settled."

Bat took hold of Runyon's right forearm and, squeezing tightly, said, "All right, but listen to me good. If you do find a connection between Peterson and one of our 'friends,' don't take it upon yourself to do anything foolish."

"Foolish? Me?" Runyon feigned wide-eyed innocence. "You mean like facing Kelly or Eastman or one of them alone? I leave that kind of foolishness to you, Bat. You're so good at it."

"Touché, Mr. Runyon, touché."

CHAPTER TWENTY-THREE

Bat spent the better part of the next day making inquiries with the people who owned the Polo Grounds, the Giants, and with the fire department.

The owners of the park and the club were not much help. They knew nothing about how the fire started. They were just grateful that it hadn't destroyed the Giants' season. They didn't want to dwell on what had happened last year. The park had since been rebuilt, and they were concerned only with the new season that was at hand.

Among the people Bat interviewed were New York Giants pitcher Rube Marquard and the manager, John J. McGraw, but neither man was able to shed any light on the situation for him. They knew very little about the fire itself. All they could tell him was that their pennant hopes had brightened considerably when they'd moved back into the friendly confines of a rebuilt Polo Grounds in early September. From that point on they had gone on to win twenty of their last twenty-four games and decimate the league the remainder of the year. (They lost the World Series to Connie Mack's Philadelphia Athletics in six games, but neither they nor Bat mentioned this fact during their conversations.)

Bat tried to locate the fire chief who had responded, but discovered that the man had retired soon after the fire and dropped out of sight. The firemen who had responded had all been transferred during the past year and were now scattered throughout the city. To track them down would have taken weeks, and he decided to put it off until he found out what Damon Runyon had learned.

Of course, the convenience of the fire chief retiring and the firemen being transferred did not escape Bat. He was now convinced that the fire had been set, and that the fire department had been involved. Oh, it could have been only to the extent that they didn't try their absolute *hardest* to save the park, and hadn't declared the fire suspicious afterward. Nothing *too* illegal there, and nothing he could prove.

Toward the end of the day he was about to head for the Metropole and his meeting with Runyon when something else occurred to him. He went to the Hall of Records to look something up first.

After Bat left the fire station, one of the men took off early and left in a hurry. He reported to the man who paid him a lot of money each month that

Bat Masterson had been asking about the men who had responded to the Polo Grounds fire. The man had then given him a bonus, which the fireman happily accepted. This was the first time in a year that he had done anything for that monthly stipend he received in the mail, and he felt better for it.

After all, a man doesn't want to be paid for doing nothing, does he?

On the way home the fireman was attacked by two men as he was passing an alley. He was dragged inside, beaten and robbed, and then one of his assailants bent over him while he was unconscious and cut his throat.

His services were no longer required.

Damon Runyon had unearthed the last address of Sam Peterson, but when he visited it he was informed that the Peterson family had moved the year before. When? Why, right after he died in that horrible fire at the Polo Grounds.

What a coincidence. Where had the grieving widow come up with enough money to move so soon afterward? he wondered.

Peterson had not worked for the Polo Grounds. Rather he had been employed by a company who supplied workmen to the park, and to other businesses as well. Very often, a man at that company—Workmen, Ltd.—told him, the men never worked in the same place two days in a row. Wasn't it rotten luck that Peterson happened to be working at the Polo Grounds that particular night? Runyon agreed that it was.

He asked the man at Workmen, Ltd., what Peterson had been doing at the park that late at night, but the man didn't know. Very often, he said, they didn't know what their men would be doing. They would simply get a request for a man, or men, to report to a certain location, and the men would be given their jobs then.

As the end of the day approached, Runyon knew little more than he had when the day started. He was about to go to the Metropole to meet with Bat when a thought suddenly struck him and he went back to Workmen, Ltd. The man on the desk there had not wanted to go along with his request, but some money changed hands and Runyon was quickly shown Sam Peterson's old records.

That done—and Runyon somewhat happier for having thought of it—he headed for the Metropole to meet with Bat.

After Damon Runyon left Workmen, Ltd., the second time, a man who worked in the office—but not the man Runyon had paid—left work early and reported to a man who paid him a sum of money each month to keep his ears open. He reported that Damon Runyon had been at the office and had bribed one of the men to show him Sam Peterson's old records, the ones that listed all the different places he had worked while employed by Workmen, Ltd.

The man was given a bonus for his information, but on the way home he was robbed and killed, as his services were no longer required.

At the Metropole, Bat and Runyon once again compared notes, each displaying an overabundance of eagerness to talk first.

"All right, all right," Bat finally said, conceding the point to Runyon. "You go first."

Runyon explained about Peterson's family moving so soon after the man's death, and concluded that the woman must have been paid off after her husband's death.

"She must have decided that a payoff was better than getting killed, so she took her children and disappeared," Runyon finished.

"That jibes with what I found out," Bat said, and he explained that virtually the entire fire company that had responded had been split up transferred all over the city and the fire chief had retired.

"Sure," Runyon said, "with a big payoff in his pocket."

"No doubt."

"Well, I went to the people Peterson worked for—he didn't work for the Polo Grounds—"

"I found that out."

"Good, then I don't have to explain that part. I went to Workmen, Ltd., Bat, and after paying one of the clerks I got a list of the places Peterson worked during the three months he was employed there." Runyon took out of his pocket the piece of paper he'd written the names on and set it down on the table. "He hardly ever worked at the same place twice, Bat, but he was a repeater at quite a few of them. If we can match any of these businesses up with those owned by Kelly, Eastman, Rosenthal—"

"I'm way ahead of you," Bat said, taking out a piece of paper of his own. "On here I have the name of the construction company that was hired to rebuild the Polo Grounds. It was a huge job, Al. You wouldn't believe the money they were paid."

"Enough to make up for all the payoffs they made?"

"More than enough."

"What's the name of the company?"

"Delores Construction Company."

Runyon quickly scanned his list and said excitedly, "It's here . . . and here . . . and here again. Bat, it's the company he worked for the most."

"I wonder why they didn't just hire him on permanently?"

"Who knows? Maybe they didn't want one of their regular men involved. This fella was a family man, Bat. They must have offered him enough money to set him up for life."

"Sure, and he died for it."

"Well, now all we have to do is find out who owns Delores Construction."

"I already did."

"Well?"

"It's owned by a company called Consolidated Companies."

Runyon frowned and said, "That's not here."

"Would you like to know who owns Consolidated Companies?"

"Definitely."

"Some other company called Integrated Businesses."

"God, how many companies are involved in that chain?"

"Enough," Bat said, pushing the paper over to Runyon's side of the table, "and a lot of them are just dummy companies, but the only one that really counts is the one up on the top of the list. It owns all of the rest."

Runyon hastily turned the list around so he could read it, then looked at Bat and said, "H&R Construction!"

Bat nodded.

"Owned and operated by one Herman Rosenthal."

CHAPTER TWENTY-FOUR

After talking it out for a long time, they decided to go to Lieutenant Charles Becker with the information. Once again Runyon waited at Palmer's while Bat went in to talk to his friend the lieutenant.

When Bat appeared in his doorway, Becker looked up, nodded, and said, "Bat."

"Hello, Charles."

"From the look on your face I'd say you have something fairly serious to talk about."

"I have."

"Take a seat, then, and let's get to it."

Bat sat across from Becker and said, "It's about Delaney Jones's death."

"What about it?"

"I believe he was killed by—or by order of—Herman Rosenthal."

"Bat, you thought that months ago."

"I thought it was a possibility, but now I'm damn sure of it."

"And just what is it that makes you so damn sure?"

Bat told him.

He told him about the cover-up of the arson at the Polo Grounds, and how Rosenthal had set the fire—or, more to point, had it set—so that his construction company would get the huge contract to rebuild it. He told him how the dead man's family had been bought off and sent packing, the same way the fire chief had; how Delaney Jones had obviously found out about it and tried blackmailing Rosenthal, who had probably given in for a while until the demands became unreasonable.

"And at that point he had Delaney Jones killed," Becker finished.

"Right."

"Prove it."

"I—"

"Prove to me that Herman Rosenthal had anything to do with the fire other than rebuilding the park."

"I—"

"Prove that he paid *anyone* off, least of all a fire chief and a grieving widow."

"You know as well as I do that money can ease—"

"Bat, you've got a lot of supposition here."

"Is that a law word?"

"It is. It means that you're saying 'Suppose this happened and suppose that happened' but you haven't got a shred of proof to back any of it up."

Bat, faced with the prospect of having his and Runyon's detective work proved useless, argued: "Come on, Charles, there must be something you can do with all of this."

"Tell me how you think Milly Cabot's death figures into it."

"Oh, that. Well, Milly and Delaney Jones were . . . involved."

"Are you telling me that Inkspot Jones was having an affair?"

"Maybe not. It's possible that they were just friends."

"Sure, tell me about it. How about telling me why she was killed?"

Bat hesitated, then took Inkspot's article out of his pocket and passed it to Becker. "Over this."

"Over this." Becker's tone was disbelieving as he sat back and read the article. When he was done, he dropped it to the desk and rubbed both hands over his face.

"I think Inkspot gave this to her to hold on to and who knows what else, but her rooms were gone through before we—before I got there. If there was anything else to be found, it was gone."

"And you're basing your whole case on this. This is what sent you looking into the fire and coming up with all of these outrageous facts?"

"They're not outrageous—"

"Maybe not, Bat," Becker said, cutting him off, "but they are useless."

"They can't be! We worked damned hard getting all of this information together. There's got to be something you can do with it."

Becker seemed about to speak, but he stopped himself short, as if something had just occurred to him. "All right, Bat."

"All right what?"

"I'll see what I can do with all of this."

Bat frowned and said, "Why the change of heart?"

"Because I'd like to see Rosenthal fall, too. Maybe with this I can give him a little push, and he'll jump the rest of the way all by himself."

"Do you think so?"

"I said maybe."

"Well, it's something," Bat said, standing up.

"One thing, Bat."

"What?"

"Stay out of it now. Stay away from Rosenthal. You've dug all of this up, now let me handle it."

"Charles, why don't I—"

"Bat, you came to me with all of this, now let me do my job."

Bat paused, then said, "All right, Charles. You take it and you do what you can with it. All I ask is that you keep me informed."

"I can do that." Becker stood up and he and Bat shook hands. "You worked pretty damn hard on this, Bat. I'm going to try like hell to get you the results you want."

"I appreciate that, Charles," Bat said, and he left the office to go over to Palmer's and let Runyon know what had happened.

When Bat reached Palmer's, he ordered a beer from the bartender, played the "Wyatt Earp" game with the man again, and then joined Runyon at a small corner table.

"What happened?"

"He's going to do what he can."

"That's what he said?"

"After he did a song and dance about how I couldn't prove anything and all the information I—we—came up with was useless."

Runyon frowned and asked, "What made him change his mind?"

"I don't know exactly," Bat said, but Runyon could tell that he was bothered by his friend's sudden change of heart.

"What about those stories . . . ?"

"What stories?"

"About Becker and Rosenthal being . . . connected."

"That's never been proven."

"But what if it's true?"

Bat stared at Damon Runyon for a long moment before saying, "We'll give Lieutenant Becker enough time to do something with the information we've given him."

"And if he doesn't?"

"If he doesn't, we'll just have to pick up the hand again and play it out ourselves."

They finished their beers and got up to leave, but as they did a group of four men approached them and blocked their path. They were big men dressed in ill-fitting suits, caps, and more than slightly potted. They were also obviously thugs. It ran through Bat's mind that perhaps they'd been sent by Rosenthal, but he thought it was too early for that.

"The bartender," one man said, "he told me you was Wyatt Earp. Is that true?"

"No, it isn't," Bat said. "Now, if you'll excuse me—"

The man wouldn't excuse him, though. He put his hand on Bat's chest and pushed him back a step. Damon Runyon tensed and watched Bat carefully.

"Why did he tell me you was?"

"He made a mistake."

"I don't think he made a mistake," the man said, becoming insistent. "You're a pretty old geezer, but I think you're Wyatt Earp. I always wanted to meet one of you living legends."

"Oh, why?"

"I wanna show my buddies here that I'm as good as any legend."

"Is that so?"

"Yeah. You wearin' a gun, Mr. Wyatt Earp?"

"Are you?"

"Yeah, I am."

"Then the only way you're going to find out if I am is to go for yours."

"Huh? You mean draw on you?"

"Of course. You do have a gun, don't you? I don't want to be arrested for shooting an unarmed man."

"I have a gun, but that wasn't what I was talking about."

"What did you have in mind, then?"

The man grinned, showing gaps in his teeth, and said, "I was gonna beat you into the floor with my fists."

"Well, we can't have that, now, can we? How would it look if a legend just stood here and let you do that? No, I'll have to insist you go for your gun."

"My gun, huh?"

"Yes."

Runyon watched, puzzled, as Bat assumed an exaggerated gunman's stance, holding his left arm away from his body.

"Hey," the dimwitted thug said, "I didn't know you was left-handed."

"You didn't? Keep your eye on my left hand, friend, and you'll see. . . ."

Bat's left hand suddenly became the center of attraction in the quiet bar. Even Damon Runyon—who knew Bat was right-handed—found himself watching it and almost missed the movement of Bat's right hand as it came out from behind him, traveled in a downward arc, and brought his empty beer mug crashing against the side of the thug's head. The big man crumpled to the floor without so much as a grunt, and his friends stared at him in shock.

"Anyone else?" Bat asked.

The other three men exchanged glances, then slowly parted to let Bat and Runyon pass.

As they reached the street, Bat grabbed for Runyon's right arm and held on to it to steady himself.

"You're not wearing that gun anymore, are you?" Runyon asked.

"No."

"You took a big chance in there."

Beginning to regain control of himself, Bat looked at Runyon and said, "I couldn't let that man beat Wyatt Earp into the floor. Wyatt would have never forgiven me."

"Bat . . ." Runyon said, shaking his head.

Bat Masterson released his hold on Runyon's arm and they walked down the street together, his legs retaining only a hint of the weakness they'd felt inside the bar.

It was just as well that they were leaving the murders in the hands of Becker for a while, he thought. He definitely needed a rest!

As Bat left his office, Lieutenant Charles Becker picked up his phone. When it was answered at the other end, he said, "We have to talk."

CHAPTER TWENTY-FIVE

Charles Becker's meeting with Herman Rosenthal was anything but amiable. Once partners, the two had been fighting like cats and dogs for the past few months, and both men could feel the situation coming to a head.

Becker visited Rosenthal's Fourteenth Street residence late that night, confident that he hadn't been seen entering. A back door had been left open for him, and he mounted the steps to the second floor, where his knock was answered by Kramer, Rosenthal's right-hand man.

Kramer and Becker exchanged no words as the policeman entered.

"Charles, so nice of you to come," Rosenthal said from behind his desk. He had not bothered to stand.

"Cut the niceties, Herman." He moved so that he was standing opposite Rosenthal across his desk, and didn't bother to sit.

"Very well. I'm glad you called, actually."

"Why is that?"

"Because I was about to call you."

"About what?"

"Your friend, Bat Masterson, and his friend, Damon Runyon, have been meddling in my affairs."

"They're doing more than just meddling, Herman. They're getting close to nailing you to the wall for murder. If Masterson had any investigative training at all, you'd be in jail right now."

"Mr. Rosenthal don't like that kind of talk," Kramer said from the side.

He was actually out of Becker's line of sight, but the lieutenant didn't bother to turn.

"Put the muzzle back on your trained dog, Herman."

"I don't know why you two can't get along," Rosenthal said, but he made no attempt to reprimand his man. "Tell me why you're here, Charles."

"For the same reason you were going to call me. Masterson and Runyon."

"They're becoming bothersome, I must admit."

"Well, don't let them go the way of a lot of other people who have been bothersome to you."

"You're telling me not to kill them?" Rosenthal frowned, not one who enjoyed being *told* anything.

"I'm telling you not to kill them, the way you killed Delaney Jones and his friend Milly Cabot."

"Milly Cabot?" Rosenthal frowned as if trying to recall the name. "Do we know a Milly Cabot, Kramer?"

"I know a whore named Milly," Kramer said. "She gives a great French—"

"Never mind, Kramer," Rosenthal said. To Becker he said, "I'm afraid we don't know a Milly Cabot."

"You may not know her, Herman, but you had her killed. I'm telling you to stay clear of Bat Masterson. I'll take care of him."

"Is that so? He's your friend, isn't he?"

"So?"

"I think we'd do better to let Kramer here take care of Mr. Masterson, and Mr. Runyon as well."

Becker pointed his right forefinger at Rosenthal and said, "If you send this ape after them, Rosenthal, I'll put *him* away and then I'll come after you."

Rosenthal's eyes narrowed and he said, "I don't like that kind of talk either, Lieutenant."

"I don't give a good goddamn what you like, Rosenthal! It was a bad idea to kill Jones and a worse one to kill the woman. Now it's all coming back at you."

"That's no way to talk to your partner, Charles."

"You're starting to tilt over, Herman, and I don't think I'm gonna be there when you land. In fact, I might even give you the final push. I think our business arrangement is just about over."

Rosenthal stared at Becker hard and then said, "I'd advise you to think that rather rash statement over a bit, Charles."

"Listen to me, Herman. I've managed to get Masterson to back off of you."

"And Mr. Runyon?"

Becker made an impatient gesture with his right hand and said, "He just does what Bat tells him to do."

"All right then, how did you manage to persuade Mr. Masterson?"

"He gave me all the facts he'd dug up—starting with the fire at the Polo Grounds." He saw Rosenthal develop a twitch in his left eye as he mentioned the Polo Grounds. "I told him I'd take care of you myself if he gave me some time."

"And what do you intend to do?"

"Keep you two away from each other."

Rosenthal relented a bit and said, "That doesn't sound like such a bad idea."

"But it goes for your trained monkey, too, or any of his friends. Let me handle this, Herman, and maybe we can go on being partners."

"Do you really think so?"

Becker moved toward the door and said, "Just sit tight for a while. I'm going to drag it out as long as I can, and maybe Masterson will lose interest."

"Of course, Charles. Whatever you say. By the way, how is your case against Zelig progressing? Have you come up with another witness?"

"My case against Zelig is none of your business, Rosenthal," Becker said. "You just better hope I don't decide to make you my pet project."

Becker stopped directly in front of Kramer, who was blocking the door. The big man looked over at Rosenthal, who nodded, and then Kramer stepped aside. He did not, however, bother to open the door for the lieutenant. Becker opened it, walked through it, and slammed it behind him. They could hear his angry footsteps progressing down the hall until he got to the steps, where they faded out.

"I think our Lieutenant Becker's usefulness has just about come to an end," Rosenthal said to Kramer.

"Does that mean I can have him?" Kramer's tone matched the look on his face—eager.

"No, I don't think so, Kramer. I have something else in mind for Lieutenant Becker. A surprise, you might say. Yes, that's it." Rosenthal looked exceedingly satisfied with himself as he repeated, "A surprise."

As Becker returned downtown, he knew that his association with Rosenthal—one very probably doomed right from the start—had finally come to an end. He didn't know if he'd be able to pin Bat Masterson's case on him, but he was going to try, right after he put Zelig away. Zelig was bigger than Herman Rosenthal, and Becker was sure that he would be able to handle Rosenthal when the time came—especially if he had Zelig's help. Although Rosenthal was the smaller fish, Becker had no solid evidence against the man, and if he wanted to, Rosenthal could hurt him. He had to handle him carefully so that he wouldn't get burned himself while trying to bring the man down. He thought that by the end of June he'd have enough on Zelig even without his dead witness, and then maybe he could turn Zelig against Rosenthal with certain promises, promises that he didn't necessarily have to keep.

He only hoped that Bat Masterson wouldn't get impatient. He'd never quite realized before how much he liked the old legend, and he didn't want him to come to any harm.

Be patient, Bat, just be a little patient. I've almost got all my cards for this hand.

Bat Masterson was already impatient.

As he fitted the key into his door, he wondered if he'd done the right thing turning everything over to Becker. Maybe he and Runyon should have kept on digging a little deeper. In the back of his mind he thought about what Runyon had said about the stories linking Rosenthal and Becker. He would have hated to find out that they were true, but then again he really wouldn't have been surprised. Becker was an opportunist, and Bat was sure that he'd bent the law more than once to suit himself, but he had never held that against him. Bat liked the man, although he wasn't quite sure whether or not they were friends. In the beginning the younger man had seemed in awe of the infamous older one, eager to hear stories of the Old West, but of late that seemed to be wearing off.

On the other hand, although Bat still wanted to see the killer of his friend —and of Milly Cabot—punished, he was growing weary of the whole affair, and would have been satisfied to have Becker write "thirty" to it.

As he entered, Emma appeared and took his jacket from him. "There's coffee on the stove."

"Good."

He sat slumped at the table while she poured him a cup and set it down in front of him.

"What happened?"

He sipped the hot coffee before answering, burning his tongue. "I spoke to Becker, told him everything we had found out and theorized."

"And?"

He took another sip of coffee, more carefully executed this time. "He's going to see what he can do with it."

"Then your part is finished?"

When he didn't answer right away, she prompted him. "Bat?"

"Yes, it is."

"Good."

"For now."

"Bat—"

"Don't worry, Emma. Becker should be able to get to Rosenthal sooner or later."

"Maybe, but are you willing to wait until later?"

Bat didn't answer.

"I'll tell *you* the answer to that one, my dear stubborn husband—no!"

"Go to bed, Emma. I'll be along soon."

Emma Masterson stood up, walked around behind her husband, bent and kissed him lovingly on the cheek, and said, "The great detective."

Her tone was hard to read, he thought, as she left the room. Either she was teasing him or was very proud of him, and it would be just like her to leave him to figure out for himself which it was.

Section Five

Damon Runyon, Gun-Toter?

There was a time in this country when men could be found who would bet their eyeballs out, and yours, too.

—Bat Masterson, September 14, 1921
The New York Morning Telegraph

CHAPTER TWENTY-SIX

May 1912

May was uneventful, for the most part.

The Giants got off to a fairly good start, behind the arms of Mathewson and Marquard.

There was talk of Arizona's becoming the forty-eighth state.

U.S. troops were forced to land in Cuba to protect the lives and property of American citizens.

Western Union and Western Electric developed a multiplex telegraph. That meant that as many as eight messages could be sent over one wire at the same time.

The U.S.S. *Jupiter*, America's first electric ship, was launched.

"Animal dances" became popular, among them the fox-trot, camel walk, chicken scratch, and bunny hug.

In spite of all this, the month was uneventful for Bat Masterson and Damon Runyon. They each wrote their respective columns, gambled a bit, drank at the Metropole with the rest of their as yet unnamed club . . . and waited in vain for word from Lieutenant Charles Becker.

Damon Runyon was out of town, traveling with the New York Giants on their current road trip, when Bat decided to go to see Charles Becker and find out what his progress was.

When Bat reached Becker's office, he found the door closed and locked. He attracted the attention of a passing patrolman, introduced himself, and asked him where Becker was.

"The lieutenant hasn't been in for days, sir."

"Is he sick?"

"No, sir, not that I know of."

"Then why hasn't he been in?"

"Most of us haven't really been let in on it, sir," the patrolman said, then lowered his voice and added, "Confidentially, I hear he's working on a case involving the arrest of some major crime figures."

That could have meant Herman Rosenthal, among others, but for some reason Bat doubted it. He thanked the man and went looking for Val O'Farrell. The detective was nowhere to be found in the building, so he vowed to question him regarding Becker's absence that evening at the Metropole.

When Bat arrived at the Metropole, he found Val O'Farrell already in attendance, deep in conversation with Tex Rickard and Alfred Lewis. The rest of the group, for whatever reason, were not in attendance. Bat had only a short while to wait before Lewis rose to leave and, minutes later, Rickard bade him and O'Farrell good night.

"What's on your mind?" O'Farrell asked.

"What makes you think I've got something on my mind?"

"You've been champing at the bit ever since you sat down."

"Guess you are a good detective, at that."

"Doesn't take a good detective to figure out what's bothering you."

"Oh?"

"You can't find your friend Becker."

"How did you know—"

"I told you it wasn't hard, but even if I wasn't a good detective, one of the men told me you were by earlier today, looking for Becker and then for me."

"Where is he, Val?"

"He's safe, if that's what you're worried about."

"It's not."

"Oh, you mean you want to know what he's working on?"

"That's right."

O'Farrell shrugged and said, "As far as I know he's after Big Jack."

"Zelig?"

"That's the guy."

"Not Rosenthal?"

"Is Becker after Rosenthal?"

"He's supposed to be."

"Well, you must know that next to Zelig, Rosenthal is small potatoes, Bat."

"I know, I know . . ."

"You dug something up, didn't you?"

Bat didn't answer.

"You gave it to Rosenthal, and now he hasn't kept his end of the bargain, has he?"

"No."

"Well, as much as I don't like Rosenthal, Bat, I'd say to give Becker some time. He's as swamped with work as I am, and Big Jack Zelig takes up a lot of his time."

"I guess so," Bat replied, but O'Farrell could see the impatience growing by the second.

"Don't go off half-cocked, Bat. If you think you've got something on Rosenthal, let Becker handle it."

"What have you heard about Becker and Rosenthal?"

O'Farrell smirked and said, "What I hear about every other policeman, honest and otherwise."

"Is Becker honest?"

"You know I won't answer that, Bat. I'll give him this, though: When he wants to be, he's a damned good policeman."

It was answer enough, though. It was clear to Bat that O'Farrell felt that Becker was not totally honest. Could it be true that he was in with Rosenthal totally? Wouldn't that mean he'd suppress any evidence that might come up against Rosenthal, rather than act on it?

"I know what you're thinking, Bat, but take my advice and give it some more time."

"Stop reading my mind. You're making me feel as if I'm sitting here naked."

"Where's your partner?"

"You mean Runyon?"

O'Farrell nodded.

"He's following the Giants around on a road trip."

"He is still working on this with you, isn't he?"

"Yes."

"Wait until he comes back at least, and then try to find Becker again."

"And if I can't?"

"You'll do what you have to do, Bat. You always have, haven't you?"

"Yep, I always have."

And probably always would.

Bat knew about Rosenthal's gambling house on West Forty-fifth Street, and he decided to go there the next night and do some gambling. He didn't see Rosenthal while he was there, but he did see his man Kramer, and once he was sure that Kramer had seen him, he left.

By using some of the contacts Malcolm Wood had given him, he found out that Rosenthal was going to Belmont the day after that, so Bat showed up there. He knew the track like the back of his hand and in no time at all was able to pinpoint Rosenthal's location. He had Kramer and two other men with him, and it was Kramer who tapped him on the shoulder and pointed to Bat, who was openly watching them.

All he wanted to do was spook Rosenthal a little. Maybe the man would make a mistake, or maybe Becker would hear about it and come looking for Bat. Either way, he hoped that by showing up at these places he might force some kind of a reaction that might lead to the end of the long search for Inkspot Jones's killer.

That night, on Fourteenth Street, Kramer begged for the opportunity to kill Bat Masterson.

First, he felt that it would solidify his position with Rosenthal, and second, it appealed to him to think that he might be the man to put an end to the legend. It didn't even bother him that he wouldn't be able to boast of the deed—except in certain circles, of course.

"First the club and then the track," he told his boss. "That's twice in two days, boss. That ain't no coincidence, and you know it."

"Relax yourself, Kramer." Rosenthal was perfectly calm, sitting behind his desk and carefully lighting a Havana cigar. When he had it going to his satisfaction, he smiled at it, stuck it in his mouth, and looked at his man. "You're doing just what he wants you to do. You're getting nervous. That's the only reason he's letting himself be seen around me. Don't worry, you'll be able to take care of him soon enough."

"And what about Becker? I thought you had plans for him."

"I do, Kramer, I do, but the man seems to have dropped out of sight. For his sake, I hope he's on Jack Zelig's tail, and not mine. When he resurfaces I'll take care of Lieutenant Charles Becker—that is, if Big Jack doesn't take care of him first."

CHAPTER TWENTY-SEVEN

June 1912

In June, when Runyon returned to the city with the Giants from their successful road trip, he immediately checked in with Bat at the *Telegraph* and was informed of Becker's disappearance while they lunched at Shanley's.

"Nobody's worried about him?"

"I talked to Val O'Farrell again a few days ago. It seems that Becker is in contact with Commissioner Waldo, just so somebody will know that he's still alive."

"I don't suppose we could get Waldo to relay a message to him for us?"

Bat smiled at the remark, which did not demand a reply. "I think we've rested on our laurels long enough," he said instead.

"Laurels?"

"Asses, then—which is probably what I was for thinking that Becker would go after Rosenthal."

"Then we'll go after him ourselves?"

"*I'll* go after him."

"Now, wait a minute, Bat. Why do you think I've gone along with everything you've said since we started this thing?"

"I assumed it was out of respect for my age."

Bat's "age" had little to do with it, but Runyon let the remark pass.

"It was because I knew I'd be seeing this through to the end, and that's what I intend to do—either with you or without you!"

"All right, don't get all riled up."

"You're not going to argue with me?"

"Hell, no. You'd get yourself killed without me a hell of a lot faster than you would with me—although, if things don't work out, you'll be just as dead."

"What are you planning?"

"While you've been gone I've been goosing Rosenthal a little, showing up in the same places at the same time and like that."

"How's he been reacting?"

"Calmly, I must say, but his man Kramer is getting itchy, I can tell."

"Kramer's dangerous."

"I know that, but he won't make a move without Rosenthal's okay."

"So what do we do? Continue to push?"

"Yes, but I think it's time to bet everything we have—even our eyeballs."

Bat and Runyon went to Bat's apartment, where the old gunfighter wanted to pick up the tool of his old trade. He felt that it was certainly time to start carrying it again.

He had hoped that Emma would not be at home, but she was seated at the kitchen table having a cup of tea when they entered.

"Hello, Al." She greeted Runyon warmly, having decided over the past half year that she liked the young man very much. Perhaps it was time for her to invite him and his wife over for a meal. . . .

"Hello, Emma."

"Why the early visit home today, Bat?" she asked, and Runyon could see right off that Emma Masterson knew something was up.

"I, uh, just came home to pick something up."

"I see," she said, looking down into her teacup as if she were reading the leaves. "It's in the top drawer, well oiled."

"Oiled?"

"I've been expecting this."

Bat faced her squarely, jaw jutting out, and said, "Oh, you have, have you? You've got me all figured out?"

"You've been griping and moaning for a month about your friend Becker backing out on your deal. I knew it was only a matter of time before you'd take matters into your own hands again—and I knew it would probably happen when Al got back to town."

"You're too smart for your own good, woman."

Bat turned and stalked to the dresser, taking the gun and shoulder rig from the top drawer. Examining the gun, he found that Emma had been true to her word. The gun gleamed with fresh oil, and he knew it would operate perfectly—if the need to use it arose.

"How are you going to go about it this time?" she asked while he slipped into the rig.

"For more than half a year I've been trying to be something I'm not," Bat replied, putting his jacket back on, "something certain people felt I could be."

He left no doubt as to who those "certain people" were.

"Now it's time for me to take care of this the way I took care of things in the old days."

"Rushing in like a fool, guns blazing," Emma said. "Like Dodge City and Tombstone, only this time you don't have Bill Tilghman or the Earps to back you up—and you're thirty years older!"

Runyon fidgeted nervously from foot to foot, aware that he was paling by comparison to Bat's old colleagues.

"Don't throw my age in my face, woman. There's nothing I can do about that."

Emma Masterson ignored her husband, however, and directed herself to Runyon. "I don't mean any offense to you, Al."

Runyon smiled and said, "None taken." He realized that she was simply a woman worried about her man.

"Does your wife know about this foolishness?" she asked.

"No—"

"Take my advice then, young man," she said sternly, "and tell her. Give her the right to worry about you. She's earned it, I'm sure."

"I'll tell her, Emma."

"Good. Now, get out of here, both of you. I want to finish my tea."

Runyon half expected Bat to approach his wife and exchange some sort of embrace, but the older man simply headed for the door. Runyon realized that these two people had been married long enough to know what the other was feeling and thinking. They had undoubtedly been through this scene countless times before—although, as Emma Masterson had pointed out, not for many years.

"Let's go, Al."

Outside on the street Runyon asked, "Where to first?"

"You do what Emma said. Go home and tell your wife that you're going to play gunfighter with an old fool and that you just might get killed for it."

"Bat—"

"Go ahead. I won't do anything too foolish until you get back. In fact, meet me at the Metropole tonight and we'll plan what we're going to do tomorrow."

"Plan?"

"Of course. Even when I rush headlong into something, I usually do it with some sort of plan."

Runyon had not gotten that impression from what Emma had said about Bat and Bill Tilghman and the Earps.

He started away and then stopped short. "Bat?"

"What?"

"Should I . . . carry a gun?"

"Do you know how to use one?"

"Uh, sure."

"Have you ever shot anyone?"

"No, but—"

"Have you ever shot *at* anyone?"

"Uh, no."

"Have you ever pointed a gun at anyone?"

"No."

After a moment of awkward silence, Bat said, "Ah hell, bring one. If you're gonna get killed, you might as well have a fighting chance."

Of all the times that Bat Masterson had held his friends entranced with tales of his exploits in the Old West, in the company of his friends and colleagues of that time—not only Bill Tilghman, Wyatt Earp and his brothers, but Luke Short, President Teddy Roosevelt, and even Wild Bill Hickok a time or two—there was one time when Bat had listened intently to someone else. It had been late in the evening, and most of the others had gone home, but he and Runyon and Alfred Lewis had been there, and Val O'Farrell began to talk about following—or "tailing," as he called it—people as part of his job.

Bat had felt fascinated that one man could follow another man for miles and days without the second man's being aware of it, and had listened in rapt attention while O'Farrell had virtually lectured on several different techniques for performing the perfect tail.

This, then, was what Bat and Runyon discussed at the Metropole, waiting until the others had all gone home.

"I remember," Runyon said in reply to Bat's question as to whether or not he remembered the night of Val O'Farrell's lecture.

"That's what we're going to do."

"What?"

"Follow Herman Rosenthal."

"Where?"

"Everywhere."

"You think he's going to do something that will give him away?"

"My plan is nothing so subtle as waiting for him to give himself away."

Bat had spent most of the afternoon thinking up several different plans, and had finally become most satisfied with this one.

"What then?"

"We're going to follow him until the time is right for us to give ourselves away."

"You're losing me," Runyon said with a confused shake of his head.

"I'm going to wait for an opportunity to pin Rosenthal against a wall, shove my gun up his nose, and tell him I *know* he killed Inkspot Jones!"

"You're right, there's nothing subtle about that. In fact, it's suicide! He's got Kramer with him at all times."

"That's where you come in."

"Me?"

Bat nodded. "Did you bring a gun?"

"Yes."

"Let's see it."

Runyon hauled the gun out of his jacket pocket and laid it on the table. Bat stared at it. It was a Smith & Wesson .38 Fifth Model, a hammerless revolver that was very popular with Pinkerton agents. It was small enough to be easily carried, and even had a grip safety to protect against accidental discharge.

"Where did you get that?"

"It was given to me as a gift a few years ago."

"Have you ever fired it?"

"Once or twice, but only at targets."

Bat picked it up and said, "Not much for target shooting, but it's a good gun for you."

"What did you mean about me taking care of Kramer?" Runyon asked. He swallowed hard. "You don't want me to kill him, do you?"

"No, no," Bat said, handing the gun back. "Put that away."

Runyon did so.

"All you're going to have to do is push it into his back and hold him steady while I, uh, have a talk with Rosenthal."

"Is that all?" Runyon asked doubtfully.

"Well—"

"What if he resists? Can I hit him on the head with the gun?"

"Not with that gun. It doesn't have enough weight. You'd probably damage it."

"Then what if he resists?"

"Just look scared."

"What? *Look* scared? I'll *be* scared, but what good will that do me?"

"If he thinks you're scared, he won't try anything."

"What the hell kind of logic is that?"

"The kind that keeps men alive." Bat tried to explain. "You see, the most dangerous man with a gun is a frightened man, because he could pull the trigger by accident. Without even meaning to—and believe me, nobody wants to die by accident just because some dude got a nervous twitch in his trigger finger."

"I see."

"So don't even think of bothering to try and put up a brave front. Look as scared as you feel, and he'll do whatever you tell him to do."

"I'll keep that in mind."

"Good."

"You know that neither one of them is going to take very kindly to this, Bat."

"That's what I'm counting on. Kramer will lose his temper, or Rosenthal's ego will force him into a move after I manhandle him. Either way, something will happen, and even with one foot in the grave I can handle either one of those jaspers with a gun."

He hoped.

"Oh, and one more thing."

"What now?" Runyon asked.

Bat assumed a look that was supposed to belie his words and said, "Just, uh, make sure you keep the safety off."

CHAPTER TWENTY-EIGHT

Damon Runyon, being the younger man, knew less about patience than did Bat Masterson.

Over the course of the first three nights that they followed Herman Rosenthal, it seemed to him—in his ignorance of such matters—that they could have grabbed him any number of times as he walked between his restaurant and his automobile, or between his automobile and his club, and then back again.

The point, Bat Masterson tried to explain, was to do it with a maximum of effort and danger.

"Kramer is always with him, and at times he has others," Bat explained. "But even when it's just the two of them, we've got to really surprise them, or—"

"Or what?" Bat had stopped himself short, and Runyon wanted him to finish the statement.

"Well, somebody could get hurt. We need them in an isolated place with the element of surprise completely on our side."

"All right." Runyon wiped his sweaty palms on his hands and said again, "All right."

After the first two nights, Bat realized that Rosenthal's schedule was so rigid that he and Runyon could afford to split up. One of them stayed at his Fourteenth Street restaurant, and when he left it there was no need for one of them to hastily try to find a cab to follow him—as they had done those first two nights—because he knew that the other man would be waiting at the other end, at the club on Forty-fifth Street. Sometimes, in between those two locations, Rosenthal would stop for dinner, often at the Metropole. (Bat and Runyon had already agreed that nothing would be tried around George Considine's place.)

Bat was convinced that no one could run through the same schedule night after night without deviating at least *one night,* and that was what they had to wait for.

"And what if it takes months?" Runyon asked impatiently.

"It won't."

"Weeks, then."

"It might, but I don't think it's likely. Inside a week, Al, and we'll have him." Bat's tone was more confident than he felt, but he didn't want Runyon getting *too* nervous with that gun in his hand—just a healthy amount of nervous to keep Kramer from trying anything when the time came.

And it came on the eighth day.

"Back to Fourteenth Street, Kramer," Rosenthal said that night, as he and the big man were preparing to leave the Forty-fifth Street club.

"What about the meeting?"

"What meeting?"

"You're supposed to meet with that bluecoat about Becker."

Rosenthal had forgotten. He had managed to find a patrolman who was fond of gambling and women, and he was going to try to use him against Becker. If he could get something on Becker—a patrolman as a witness to a payoff would be ideal—he'd be able to keep the lieutenant in line.

"All right. Where are we supposed to meet?"

"A building on Forty-eighth."

Rosenthal frowned. "No point in taking the car, then. We'll walk the three blocks."

"I don't think that's a good idea—" Kramer began to protest.

"Don't be an old woman, Kramer," Rosenthal said. "Let's go."

The big man shrugged his massive shoulders and followed his boss to the front door.

"Here he comes," Runyon said, fighting back a yawn. They were in a deep, darkened doorway across the street, which they had been using as cover for a week. "Back to Fourteenth Street, no doubt, and then we can get something to eat—"

"Look!" Bat's voice was a low, excited hiss as he saw Rosenthal and the hulking Kramer turn *left* instead of the customary right.

"Where are they going?" Runyon demanded.

"It doesn't matter, because they're not going to get there. Come on."

He grabbed Runyon's sleeve and virtually dragged him out of the doorway. The younger man's heart was in his throat, and his hand was on the gun in his pocket.

God, he hoped he wouldn't have to shoot anybody!

They followed along across the street for a block until they got far enough away from Rosenthal's club.

"I know this block," Bat said in a whisper. "There's an alley ahead, on the next block."

"What if they turn on the next street, Forty-seventh?"

"Then we'll take them someplace else, but this is the night, Al."

"Should we get ahead of them?"

"No, we'll take them from behind—quietly!"

They started across the street then, moving hurriedly but as silently as they could. To Bat's great satisfaction they did not turn on Forty-seventh, but continued on toward Forty-eighth.

As they reached the same side of the street, they were only yards behind the two men, and Bat put his hand against Runyon's back to indicate that now was the time. They both produced their guns and sprinted ahead.

"What—" Kramer said, the first to realize that something was amiss. He half turned and saw Runyon's face a split second before he saw the gun. The fear in Runyon's eyes froze the man solid. "Take it easy."

"What's wrong—" Rosenthal started to ask, but as he turned, Bat thrust the barrel of his Peacemaker right up against his nose.

"In the alley," Bat commanded.

"What alley?"

"This one." Bat pushed Rosenthal ahead of him, staggering the man, who regained his balance right in front of the mouth of the alley.

"Masterson?" he said as Bat stepped into the light of a nearby lamp pole. "Are you crazy?"

"Get in the alley!"

Rosenthal looked into the inky blackness of the alley, then looked past Masterson at Kramer.

The big man did not seem inclined to argue with either Masterson or Runyon. He simply looked over his shoulder at Runyon and said again, "Take it easy."

"*You* take it easy," Runyon said, jabbing the man's broad back with the barrel of his gun.

Bat reached out for Kramer's elbow and pushed him into the alley.

For a moment Bat thought that he'd made a serious mistake, one he wouldn't have made twenty years ago. It was so dark in the alley that he lost sight of Rosenthal and Kramer, and the two men could have done anything at that point—except that they couldn't see either. After a few moments he was able to make out their shapes, and he instructed them to keep walking to the back of the alley.

"All right," he said when they reached a brick wall. "Stop. Kramer, move away from your boss."

Kramer moved a few steps away, and Runyon went with him, prodding him with the gun."

"Take it easy, damn it!" Kramer hissed, and Runyon was gratified to hear a faint tinge of concern in the man's tone. Bat was right—the fact that he was scared was making the man extra careful.

He tightened his grip on the gun, his finger in the trigger guard but not quite on the trigger. He didn't trust his nerves that much yet.

"Masterson, you're making a bad mistake here," Rosenthal said menacingly.

"You made the mistake, Rosenthal, when you had Delaney Jones killed."

"Why would I have him killed?"

"To cover up the fact that you had the fire at the Polo Grounds set so that your company could get the job to rebuild it."

"That's . . . absurd." Rosenthal's denial was halfhearted, and Bat finally knew for dead sure that Rosenthal was responsible for Inkspot's death. He was sorely tempted to pull the trigger of the Peacemaker and end it right there and then, but that would have meant killing Kramer as well. He *might* have been able to do it, too, but he wasn't sure how Runyon would react, and he didn't want to put the younger man in that difficult a situation.

"Are you going to kill me?"

"I just want you to know that I could have killed you very easily, Herman."

Rosenthal frowned now, and suddenly he believed that Bat wasn't going to kill him. "Now you're compounding your mistake, Masterson. First you put your hands on me and point a gun in my face, and now you're going to let me walk away. If I was you, I'd kill me right now, because if you don't, *you're* dead."

"Bat—" Runyon said.

"Quiet." Bat never took his eyes off Rosenthal. "You don't scare me, Rosenthal. I've handled men who could chew you and your man up and spit you out for breakfast."

"That was then, old man," Rosenthal said maliciously, "and this is now. Your time has passed you by, and now you're as good as dead."

"Well then, I guess I've got nothing to lose, do I?"

For a moment Rosenthal thought he'd overplayed his hand. His eyes widened as Bat raised his gun and then brought the barrel across, slamming it into Rosenthal's jaw. The man moaned and dropped to the ground, landing in a seemingly boneless heap at Bat's feet.

Bat turned to look at Kramer then, who regarded him without expression. "What about you?"

Kramer said nothing. He didn't want to push the man into killing him—and if he walked away, he knew he'd be able to kill Masterson later.

"I know what you're thinking, Kramer. Don't let him send you after me, because next time you won't walk away."

The look on Kramer's face said he doubted it, but he remained silent.

"All right, let's go," Bat said to Runyon. To Kramer he said, "Wait ten minutes before you carry your boss out of here. If I see your head or his before then, I'll blow it off."

Kramer stood as if he were made out of stone.

Runyon moved away from the man and backed nervously out of the alley.

"When he wakes up, tell him I'm going to see that he pays for killing Delaney Jones, and the woman."

Silence.

"Yeah," Bat said, and backed out of the alley to where Runyon was waiting on the street. He put his gun away and told Runyon to do the same.

Runyon hastily tucked the gun away and asked, "Can we go now?"

"Where?"

"Anywhere. I've got to pee—bad!"

CHAPTER TWENTY-NINE

June 1912

On June 21, Lieutenant Charles Becker took Big Jack Zelig into custody, reappearing himself for the first time since Bat had spoken to him.

Bat and Runyon had been jumping at shadows of late—though Bat would never admit it—waiting for Rosenthal to make his move. The report of Zelig's arrest interested both of them, and they discussed it over lunch at Shanley's

"Maybe now Becker will go after Rosenthal," Runyon proposed.

"If he ever had any intentions of doing so." Bat's tone was doubtful. He had decided that he'd been wrong about Becker all this time and thought that their friendship was probably over.

Runyon pleaded some pressing baseball business and went back to work, leaving Bat to finish his lunch alone—until Charles Becker showed up.

Bat saw the man enter but studiously avoided looking up as the policeman approached his table.

"Hello, Bat. Mind if I sit down?"

Bat shrugged.

"Look," Becker said, seating himself, "I don't blame you for being angry."

"I'm not."

"Sure you are, but I had a chance to nail Zelig and I had to take it. I intended to go after Rosenthal right afterward, honest I did."

"Don't matter."

"It does, Bat." Becker waited a few moments to see if Bat had anything to offer, and then went on. "Look, I heard about what you did to Rosenthal last week."

"What did I do to Rosenthal?"

"You laid open his cheek with the barrel of your gun, that's what you did!" Becker said, suddenly becoming agitated.

"I did? I'm a newspaperman, Lieutenant. Why would I be doing a thing like that?"

"And you signed your own death warrant," Becker went on. "This isn't Tombstone or Dodge, Bat, and you aren't thirty damn years old!"

"You sound like my wife."

"Then she makes good sense. Rosenthal's gonna come after you, all right, and there won't be a damn thing you can do about it."

"I can take care of myself."

"Bat, I've got a lot of respect for the man you once were, but that man's gone now."

"Do tell."

"Bat, you stubborn—"

"Are you done? You're ruining my lunch."

"Your lunch? I'm ruining your lunch?" Becker's attitude was one of disbelief. "Why'd you have to go and pull a stunt like this, Bat? You ruined a whole lot more than your lunch, you know. You ruined your goddamn life— whatever you had left of it!"

"Look, you got your man," Bat said, looking at Becker for the first time, gesturing with the knife in his hand. "Don't worry about me. I'll get mine."

"If he doesn't get you first," Becker said, standing up. "And I'll tell you something sad: My money's on him!"

"Then you're backing a loser, son."

"You're a stubborn old man!" Becker turned on his heel in disgust and stalked out.

Bat regarded the remainder of his lunch with distaste and got up to get another beer.

Becker went directly from Shanley's Grill to Rosenthal's restaurant on Fourteenth Street. He barged in, stormed up the stairs, and burst into Rosenthal's office.

Herman Rosenthal was seated behind his desk, the right side of his face covered by a bandage from just below his eye to the line of his jaw. Kramer was standing next to him, and both men looked up in surprise.

"Becker," Rosenthal said. "What the hell are you doing here? Come out of hiding, did you? Oh, yes, that's right. You got Big Jack. I read about it in today's paper."

"Forget Big Jack, Rosenthal." Becker crossed the room and stopped just in front of Rosenthal's desk. "I'll make a deal with you."

"A deal? What kind of a deal?"

"I'll lay off you and I'll keep Masterson away from you."

"I see. And what's my part of this bargain?"

"Leave Masterson alone."

Rosenthal frowned. "Do you see this?" He was referring to the bandage.
Becker held out both of his hands and said, "I'll arrest him for it."
Rosenthal looked surprised. "Does he mean that much to you?"

"Never mind what he means to me. I don't want you to kill him."

"I'm afraid you don't have any say in the matter, Becker. Now, why don't you just turn around and go back out the way you came in before I have Kramer throw you out."

Before even he was aware that he was going to do it, Becker went for his gun. For a big man, Kramer moved incredibly fast, rounding the desk and catching Becker's right wrist in his massive hand before the policeman could come out with his gun.

Kramer pulled Becker's hand out of his jacket for him, and the gun dangled from fingers that were already numb from the big man's grip. Kramer shook Becker's hand like a rag, and the gun fell to the floor.

"You made a big mistake, Becker," Rosenthal said, leaning across his desk. "You should have been satisfied with your share, but you had to try and bleed me. I stood for that, though. Now you're siding with Masterson against me, and us in business together."

"Not anymore we're not," Becker said, wincing from the pain in his wrist, which still rested in Kramer's grip. "I'm going to close you down, Rosenthal, once and for all."

"Well, you cut your own income if you do that, but if that's the way you feel, then I guess we're no longer partners. Is that right?"

"It sure is."

"In that case, you don't belong in this office without some sort of warrant."

"Tell your trained monkey to let go of my wrist and I'll go."

"But you'll be back, right?"

"You better believe that."

"Kramer, show the lieutenant what a mistake it would be for him to come back here—ever!"

Kramer smiled, and before Becker could react he buried his left fist in the policeman's stomach while releasing the hold on his wrist with his right. Gagging, Becker staggered back and fell to the floor. Kramer advanced on him, and some sixth sense enabled the lieutenant to stagger to his feet to face him. As Kramer closed on him, Becker swung his right fist, but there was no power behind it. Kramer swatted it away like a fly and hit Becker in the face with his right fist. As the man started to fall, Kramer grabbed the front of his jacket with his left hand and, holding him up that way, hit him in succession one . . . two . . . three more times, and then let him fall. Bloodied, choking on his own blood, Becker could only lie there fighting for his breath, wondering if Rosenthal was going to let Kramer beat him to death.

"All right, Kramer," he heard Rosenthal's voice say, and then with great relief heard him add, "toss that sack of garbage out of here," just before he blacked out. . . .

When Kramer returned from "showing" the lieutenant out, he eyed Rosenthal balefully.

"You disapprove."

"If you don't mind my saying so, sir, you made a mistake."

"Did I?"

"You should have let me kill him."

"And tell me, Kramer, killing a policeman? That wouldn't be a mistake?"

Kramer simply shrugged his beefy shoulders, indicating that whether it was a mistake or not, it wouldn't have been any trouble as far as he was concerned.

"Still, it may become necessary," Rosenthal admitted, "depending on how the lieutenant reacts to the death of Bat Masterson."

Kramer perked up.

"Yes, Kramer, I believe the time is finally drawing near. Just let me think about it a bit."

Kramer frowned. In his experience, when Rosenthal stopped to think, he was flirting with trouble.

On the other hand, Rosenthal felt that his next move had to be thought out very carefully. In fact, killing Bat Masterson might have just the opposite effect on Lieutenant Becker. Masterson's death—along with one or two other tactics—might convince him *not* to make any trouble.

Yes, aside from Masterson's being troublesome, his death might solve not only that problem but the problem of Charles Becker as well.

And, of course, if it didn't, there was always Kramer.

He's misread me, Becker thought, picking himself up off the floor of the alley next to Rosenthal's building. He staggered and steadied himself against the nearby wall, waiting for a wave of dizziness and nausea to pass. When it did, he pushed away from the wall and began to walk.

This thing with Rosenthal had been coming to a head for a long time, but now it was the danger to Bat Masterson—a man Becker admitted only to himself whom he greatly admired—that would finally decide the fate of Herman Rosenthal.

Section Six

Dodge City, New York

The American public [is] without a doubt . . . the biggest aggregation of sapheads in the world.

—Bat Masterson, August 12, 1919
The New York Morning Telegraph

CHAPTER THIRTY

July 1912

July started like a slow-burning fuse—and no matter how slowly a fuse burns, it eventually causes an explosion. . . .

On July 1, Lieutenant Charles Becker sent his emissary, a street thug named Jack Rose, to the Tombs to speak to Big Jack Zelig on his behalf. Zelig was promised his freedom—"Evidence can be misplaced"—if he would help Becker out with a "small problem."

Zelig agreed.

On July 5, Lieutenant Charles Becker stationed a uniformed police officer outside every one of Herman Rosenthal's buildings, whether they housed restaurants or gambling establishments.

This would go on for five days.

On July 11, Herman Rosenthal went to the West Side Police Court and complained about the "harassment" he was being subjected to at the hands of Lieutenant Charles Becker. He received little satisfaction.

On July 14, Herman Rosenthal visited the offices of *The New York World* and spoke of his relationship with Charles Becker for publication. He alleged that not only Becker was on his payroll, but that they were actually "partners" in certain endeavors.

Rosenthal also made it no secret that he had a July 16 appointment to speak with District Attorney Charles S. Whitman on "certain matters." People were heard to say that Rosenthal was going to make a full disclosure before a grand jury.

This was never verified.

As of July 16, the charges were all in place and the fuses had burned almost all the way down to the powder. . . .

CHAPTER THIRTY-ONE

Bat Masterson, Damon Runyon, William Lewis, Val O'Farrell, and Tex Rickard were seated at their usual table at the Hotel Metropole when O'Farrell suddenly looked up and cleared his throat. The others turned and looked in the direction of his gaze.

"Rosenthal," Runyon said. The crime boss was followed closely by his man Kramer. Although Rosenthal never once looked Masterson's way, Kramer caught the older man's eyes and grinned tightly.

"Excuse me—" O'Farrell began, sliding his chair back to get up, but all at the table were surprised at how quickly Bat Masterson clamped a hand down on the detective's arm.

"Where are you going?"

"Just to talk to them."

"There's no need for that."

"Bat," O'Farrell said, sitting back down, "this is a potentially explosive situation here. I know you're carrying a gun, and I can guarantee you that at least Kramer is."

"No one's going to start shooting in here, Val." Bat released his friend's arm. "Please, just stay right here."

O'Farrell shrugged to the others and quietly acquiesced to his friend's request.

"At the very least," Lewis said, "you fellas oughtn't to leave here alone."

Runyon looked vaguely shocked at having been included in the statement, but then mentally berated himself. Of course, if Bat was in danger, so was he. That had been the way he'd wanted it, hadn't it?

After all, he never claimed to be all *that* smart!

Nervously, Runyon touched the gun in his pocket, which he had not drawn since that night in the alley save to put it away at night and pick it up again in the morning.

"I have a bad feeling. . . ." O'Farrell said, but he let it trail off. He realized that Rosenthal had been pushed hard recently, by both Masterson and Charles Becker. Both men were probably just waiting for Rosenthal to make his move, and tonight was probably as good a night as any, considering that the rumors had Rosenthal talking to a grand jury later that day.

It was 1:05 A.M., July 16.

Rosenthal and Kramer stayed at their table for the better part of an hour, and the tableau at Masterson's table remained the same. All of the men present were waiting and watching intently, expecting something to happen.

At 1:50 A.M. a man approached Rosenthal's table and whispered something to him. Rosenthal nodded, said something to Kramer, and pushed his chair back preparatory to getting up.

"They're leaving," William Lewis said.

Bat's chair made a scraping noise as he pushed it back slowly.

"Bat—" O'Farrell said.

"Just going out for a breath of fresh air, Val." Masterson's eyes were fixed on Rosenthal's back.

"I'll join you," Damon Runyon said, hurriedly getting to his feet.

Bat turned and looked at the younger man, seemed about to protest, and then thought better of it. "All right."

"See you later fellas," Runyon said with more cockiness than he felt.

Bat and Runyon left the table and followed in Rosenthal's wake as the crime boss and his henchman stopped at the door for a newspaper, and then walked outside.

Outside, Rosenthal stopped on the steps and looked at the newspaper headline: ROSENTHAL TO TESTIFY IN FRONT OF GRAND JURY.

He chuckled to himself, shaking his head and reading it again. He liked the way his name looked in that huge, black print.

"Boss . . ." Kramer said, as if to bring Rosenthal back to the business at hand—killing Bat Masterson.

"Yes," Rosenthal said, folding the newspaper. The grand jury would have a long wait for him. "Be ready, Kramer."

"I've been ready for this for a long time."

"Yes," Rosenthal said, "I suppose you have."

He started down the steps just as Bat Masterson and Damon Runyon came through the doors. He would hear the shots that ended their lives as he walked away.

At least, that was the plan.

The fuse struck the powder at that point, and there was an explosion.

As they exited from the Metropole, Bat saw Kramer standing on the steps, smiling, his gun already out. With his left hand he pushed Runyon out of the way, while going for his gun with his right.

God, but his hand moved slowly.

Kramer felt the tight grin on his face freeze in place. Runyon was tumbling to the side, out of the line of fire, and Masterson was reaching for his gun. The old man was fast.

As Rosenthal stepped down off the last step, beneath the canopy lights of the Metropole Hotel an automobile pulled to a stop at the curb and four men jumped out.

They all had guns and fired simultaneously into Herman Rosenthal's body.

Rosenthal just had time to feel some confusion, and astonishment, and then nothing.

Kramer's shot went wild as he rushed it, and then Masterson's gun was out. He fired once, the bullet striking the big man in the chest, and then became aware of other shots being fired.

It was like Dodge City all over again.

CHAPTER THIRTY-TWO

The "murder" of Herman Rosenthal was investigated personally by the district attorney, Charles S. Whitman.

A cabaret singer named Charles Gallagher had been passing the Metropole just as the automobile had pulled up, and amid all the shooting he had managed to see the license-plate number of the auto.

Before dawn the automobile was located and with it the owner, who had driven the car that night. He insisted to police that he had known nothing of the other men's intentions, and had simply been hired to drive. He furnished Whitman with the names of the men in the car, and the man who had hired them.

The other men in the auto had been Louis Rosenberg, also known as "Lefty Lou"; Harry Horowitz, called "Gyp the Blood"; Jack Seidenshner, known as "Whitey Lewis"; and Frank Cirofici, called "Dago Frank."

They were all known members of Big Jack Zelig's gang.

The man who had hired them was Jack Rose, who certainly had no intentions of taking the rap for Lieutenant Charles Becker.

He gave Becker to Whitman, and the lieutenant was arrested for conspiracy to commit murder.

The incident during which Bat Masterson had killed Rosenthal's man Kramer was deemed to be totally separate and apart from the conspiracy to murder Rosenthal, and Bat was found to have acted in self-defense.

Whitman had no time to waste on a newspaperman when he had a policeman to prosecute.

On the twentieth day of what had now become a relatively calm July, Bat Masterson went to the Tombs to see Lieutenant Charles Becker.

"You're a fool, you know," he told the younger man.

"That's probably right."

"How could you trade Zelig for Rosenthal?"

Becker shrugged.

It had been brought to light that Jack Rose had approached Zelig on behalf of Becker and offered him freedom if he would supply four men to be used to murder Herman Rosenthal.

"You can bet Zelig was surprised," Becker said. "I was after him for a long time."

"You didn't trade Zelig for Rosenthal, did you?" Bat's words were as much an accusation as a demand.

"What do you mean?"

"You traded him for me, or at least that was your intention."

"You're crazy."

"You had Rosenthal killed to keep him from killing me. I was right the first time—you are a fool."

Becker said, "You're crazy" again, and left it at that.

Bat stared at Becker and thought sadly, I had no idea. . . .

The four assassins and Charles Becker were found guilty on October 24, 1913, and sentenced to be executed.

On February 24, 1914, the Court of Appeals overturned Becker's conviction and granted him a new trial due to what they called "prejudicial rulings" on the part of the presiding judge, John W. Goff.

On April 13, 1914, Louis Rosenberg, Harry Horowitz, Jacob Seidenshner, and Frank Cirofici were executed at Sing Sing prison.

On May 5, 1914, Lieutenant Charles Becker was again found guilty by a jury.

On July 30, 1915, Charles Becker was executed.

Epilogue

CHAPTER THIRTY-THREE

"How could you have known that Becker felt that way about you?" Damon Runyon asked Bat over a drink at the Metropole. It was shortly after Bat had spoken to Becker at the Tombs. "I'd only seen him snap at you for interfering in police business."

"That was his job. I forgot . . ."

"What?"

"Nothing."

Bat forgot that a man's job had nothing to do with his friends.

"Do you think he's guilty?" Runyon asked. "That he really did it?"

Bat thought it over a moment, then said, "Yes."

"But what about Inkspot, and the woman, Milly Cabot? How will we know who killed them?"

"We know. I told Ida that Rosenthal was responsible, and that Kramer was probably the one who actually killed Inkspot."

"And was she satisfied?"

"As satisfied as a woman can be without her husband around."

"But how can we be sure, Bat, now that they're both dead? What if Becker's the one who—"

"Don't even think it." Bat's tone stopped Runyon cold. "Becker may not have been the most honest policeman, but he was a good one. He wouldn't have killed Inkspot, not to cover up for Rosenthal."

"If you say so," Runyon said, prudently deciding not to press the point.

Bat went home that night and had dinner with Emma. She told him that she had seen Ida Jones that day.

"She's very grateful to you, Bat."

"I didn't do anything."

"Of course you did. Oh, you might have done it all wrong—" She paused long enough to enjoy his startled look, then went on, "But look how it came out. Inkspot's killer has been punished."

"And what about Charles Becker?"

Emma Masterson moved around behind her husband and put her hands on his shoulders. "You didn't ask him to do what he did."

"I never suspected that he would, or I would have stopped him. I misjudged him, Emma. He was more of a friend than I could ever have been."

"You saw him today, didn't you?"

"Yes."

"Was he complaining? Crying? Lamenting?"

"None of those."

"In an odd way, Bat, he might even be satisfied with the way things came out."

There was that word again.

"Satisfied," Bat said beneath his breath. "How could anyone be satisfied?"

The entire affair had started with the disappearance and death of a friend, he thought, and damned if it hadn't ended with the death of another.

Bat Masterson wasn't satisfied.

Not by a damn sight!

Author's Notes

The attempted fix of the Jim Flynn–Carl Morris fight and Bat's successful efforts to prevent it are fact.

The shooting death of Herman Rosenthal on the steps of the Metropole is fact, as are the fates of the men involved.

Everything that occurred between these two incidents is pure fabrication, the author's picture of how these two incidents might possibly have been connected. There is no evidence to indicate that they actually were anything but two separate and distinct occurrences.

Many of the names that appear in this story are real, but the author in no way claims that the true character and personality of these people are accurately depicted here.

The author's main goal in the preceding pages was to show a "different" Bat Masterson than popular history does. It is fact that Bat Masterson became a sportswriter in New York City and eventually rose to the vice-presidency of *The New York Morning Telegraph*.

The author has tremendous respect for a man, a legend of the Old West, who could turn his life around when the Old West died out and carve a place for himself in history as something other than a "gunman" or a "gambler."

This story was intended as a homage to Bat Masterson.

Bibliography

Bat Masterson: The Man and the Legend, by Robert K. DeArment (University of Oklahoma Press, 1979).

Bat Masterson, by Richard O'Connor (Doubleday, 1957).

The Damon Runyon Story, by Ed Weiner (Longmans, Green & Co., 1948).

The Great Gunfighters of the West, by Carl Breihan (NAL, 1977).

The Mob: 200 Years of Organized Crime in New York, by Virgil W. Peterson (Green Hill Publishers, 1983).

The Timetables of American History, Lawrence Urdang, editor (Simon & Schuster, 1981).

Brooklyn . . . and How It Got That Way, by David W. McCullough (The Dial Press, 1983).

Nineteenth Century New York in Rare Photographic Views, Frederick S. Lightfoot, editor (Dover, 1981).

New York 1900, by Robert A. M. Stern, Gregory Gilmartin, and John Massengale (Rizzoli, 1983).

The Architecture of New York City, by Donald Martin Reynolds (Macmillan, 1984).

Times Square: A Pictorial History, by Jill Stone (Macmillan 1982).

New York Landmarks, Alan Burnham, A.I.A., editor (Wesleyan University Press, 1963).

The Sports Encyclopedia: Baseball, by David S. Neft and Richard M. Cohen (St. Martin's Press, 1985 Edition).

Acknowledgments

Since this is my most ambitious work to date, and probably my best, certain people should be acknowledged.

First, all of the people who have ever edited or worked on my westerns. They all have a small part of this one:

Michael Seidman, Greg Tobin, Damaris Rowland, Linda Smith, Judith Riven, Joe Blades, John Douglas, Chris Miller, Nancy Parent . . . and Pat LoBrutto, who has a *big* piece of this.

Next, my friends and colleagues whose advice, encouragement, enthusiasm, and works helped me along the way:

Max Allan Collins, Loren D. Estleman, Ed Gorman, Mike Madonna, Bill Pronzini, Jory Sherman, as well as Michael Seidman and Pat LoBrutto—both of whom made both of these lists—and Dale Walker, who offered me some material I never got a chance to make use of. The offer was appreciated, Decatur.

And, last but not least, my agent, Dominick Abel, because he has always believed in me.

In one way or another, all of the above people were there along the way, and for that I thank them.